REALITY TV 101:

no one ever promised reality meant real.

dating the DILF

USA TODAY BESTSELLING AUTHOR

AMALI ROSE

Dating the DILF
Copyright © 2019 by Amali Rose

This book is a work of fiction. Names and characters, places, and incidents are the product of the author's imagination or are used fictitiously. Any resemblance to actual events, locales, or persons, living or dead, is coincidental.

Editing: Ellie McLove - My Brother's Editor
Proofreading: Judy Zweifel - Judy's Proofreading
Cover Design: Ben Ellis – Tall Story Designs
Cover Image: Adobestock

All rights reserved. In accordance with the U.S. Copyright Act of 1976, electronic sharing of any part of this book without the permission of the publisher or author constitute unlawful piracy and theft of the author's intellectual property. If you would like to use the material from this book (other than for review purposes), prior written permission must be obtained by contacting the publisher at authoramalirose@gmail.com. Thank you for your support of the author's rights.

FBI Anti-Piracy Warning:

The unauthorized reproduction or distribution of a copyrighted work is illegal. Criminal copyright infringement, including infringement without monetary gain, is investigated by the FBI, and is punishable by up to five years in prison, and a fine of $250,000.

dating the DILF

This book is for Rachel.
You are kindness and loyalty personified.
Thank you for putting up with me.

*"My wish for you is that you continue.
Continue to be who and how you are, to astonish a mean
world with your acts of kindness."*

Maya Angelou

SYNOPSIS:

After a hilarious meet cute involving ice cream, too-tight pants and a bit of bottom flashing, this single dad and career-driven woman just might have found their match....

Charlotte and Miles have everything going against them.
He's running from a reality TV scandal, while she's running from a painful childhood.
He has an adorable toddler with an unfortunate potty mouth, while children were never part of her plan.
And, maybe the most significant obstacle of them all... he hates ice cream, and she's addicted to it.

But, the heart and brain often long for different things. Can they beat the odds and find their happily ever after?

CHAPTER ONE

CHARLOTTE

My eye twitches as an unmistakable aroma fills my office and my nose perks up, ready to hunt down the source with speed and efficiency that would rival a bloodhound. Because what the *actual* fuck.

I'm on my feet before I have a chance to second-guess myself, and when I cross the threshold into my outer office, I have to tamp down a snarl.

"What is that?" I hiss.

Adelaide, my assistant, freezes, her hand halfway to her mouth and her eyes wide. Taking a moment to compose herself, she exhales a quiet breath as though preparing herself to go to battle.

"It goes by many names, Charlie." She furrows her brows, considering me seriously. "Java, Joe, Jitter Juice, Energy Infusion, Rocket Fuel… but I generally refer to it as coffee." She draws the word coffee out slowly, before wrapping both her hands around the paper cup and lifting it to her mouth and taking a long sip.

I bend down, squaring my hands on her desk, and lean forward. The delicious hazelnut scent is practically screaming my name, begging me to come closer. Which I do, much to Adelaide's horror, who is about to topple backward as she attempts to put distance between us.

"I thought we were giving up coffee?" My voice comes out as an annoying whine, and if I was paying attention to anything other than the delicious nectar in her hands, I'd probably hate myself a little for that pathetic display. But my two-day-caffeine-free brain is far too distracted.

"Oh," she startles. "I mean I kind of assumed the *we* part was more rhetorical. I figured my part of the 'we' was more cheerleader-esque. You know, to support *you* to give it up, because…" She pauses to take another sip of her drink, her eyes rolling back in an excessive display of coffee-induced ecstasy that I really don't appreciate. "I don't want to."

I stand upright, silently pondering where I could hide a body. More specifically Adelaide's body. She's pretty small, so it wouldn't need to be a large space. Perhaps in that manky storage cupboard up on the sixteenth floor? Nobody ever uses it. Of course, I do need her for the Thompson meeting at eleven, so taking her out would have to wait until after that…

"Charlie!" Adelaide flips her long blonde hair over her shoulder and glares at me in exasperation. "You're planning my murder again, aren't you?"

"I don't know what you're talking about." Dragging

my eyes away from the coffee in her hand, I pin her with a look of, what I hope is, polite indifference.

"You look constipated, stop that." She smirks at me and I slump down, leaning against her desk and sighing with defeat.

"Can you get me a coffee, please. An Americano with two extra shots."

"I'm sorry, what? I didn't quite catch that." Adelaide turns her head to the side and lifts her ear in my direction. My jaw starts to ache, and I realize I'm clenching my teeth.

"Go and get me a coffee, Addy, before I fire your ass for being literally the worst cheerleader in the whole goddamn world."

I head back to my office with her laughter ringing in my ears and settle myself back behind my desk just as the internal phone line rings.

"Charlotte Reed."

"Charlotte, Mr. Erickson wants you to meet him and Kendall at seven tonight, to go over the Ultra Bond acquisition with them." My boss' no-nonsense assistant brusquely greets me. "Their plane gets in from New York at six and they'll come here directly."

I hold in a groan, knowing there is no way Louis and Kendall will make it here by seven and I have lost any chance I had of getting out of here before nine tonight.

"Of course, Helen. Conference room three?"

Minutes later I am pulling up the Ultra Bond file to make sure everything is ready for tonight, when Adelaide walks in holding a steaming coffee cup and a small bag that promises some kind of pastry deliciousness.

"I got you a cheese danish while I was there." She throws the bag on my desk and hands me the cup before grinning at me. "Tim says hi, by the way."

I ignore her, and the third-degree burns I'm currently inflicting on my throat as I gulp down my coffee.

"I *said,* Tim said hi." Adelaide's usually melodic southern drawl takes on an annoying lilt.

"That's nice." Tim is one of the young—emphasis on young—men who work on the coffee cart that makes the rounds through our offices. He might possibly have a small crush on me, and he really is very sweet, but I haven't been interested in college boys since I was *in* college.

Adelaide flops into the chair opposite my desk while I lean back in my own chair and quirk a questioning brow at her.

"I'm pretty sure you're supposed to be preparing an affidavit for me right now." I tuck a strand of my brown hair back into the ponytail it has come loose from.

"You were the one who interrupted me, but whatever. Just hear me out." I sigh, resignedly, and give her a nod to continue, knowing she won't let this drop until I do. "I know he's young, but he's legal."

I wait for her to go on, but she gives me nothing else.

"That's it?" I snort. "That's your whole spiel?"

"Well, he's also hot, but I thought even you could see that." She shrugs carelessly.

"I don't have time for 'hot,'" I argue.

"Make time for it! Slut it up all cougar-like and get in that boy's boxers. Your vagina will thank you." Addy laughs.

I bite my lip to disguise a smile. "It's not that simple. If I want to make junior partner in the next couple of years, I don't have time for relationships." I move my chair forward, ignoring Adelaide's groan, and begin rifling through the paperwork on my desk. "Which reminds me, Louis and Kendall want to be briefed on the UB acquisition tonight." I hand her a pile of papers. "Can you make me copies of this report before you get back to the affidavit?"

"What time did you get here this morning?"

I blink slowly a couple of times, considering her question. "Six-thirty, why?"

"Six-thirty." She shakes her head and I already know I'm not going to like where this is going. "And after this meeting tonight, you'll get out of here at, what? Nine, nine-thirty?"

"What's your point, Addy?"

"That's a fifteen-hour day. And you're doing that more and more often lately. Not to mention you're here most weekends."

Every weekend, but that seems ill-suited to my argument right now.

"It's the job, you know that as well as I do."

"Do you like the job?" Her question stops me short

and I try to come up with an answer that will pacify her.

"It's a good job. It has great benefits, it's secure and the pay is—"

"Do. You. *Like* it?" She bites her lip and levels me with an exasperated look. "Are you passionate about it? Does it fill you up?"

This right here is why you should never work with your friends.

"I'm passionate about the law," I defend myself.

"You're passionate about negotiating deals so rich assholes can become even richer assholes?" Her voice oozes disbelief.

"I need—"

"You need to get laid." It's said with a roll of her eyes and it's the final straw.

"I need security," I snap. "I need to know that I have the resources to take care of myself and provide for myself. If you have a problem with that, then I'm sorry, but I also don't really care."

"Okay, okay." She holds up her hands in surrender. "I'm sorry, I know this job is important to you. I just want you to remember that it's not the *only* important thing." She stands and smooths down her skirt. "Life can be so much more than what you're making of it, Charlie. Love and relationships don't have to mean you lose something. Sometimes they're the reason you *get* everything."

I watch her walk out, her words hanging heavy in the air, before I turn to my computer and get back to work.

The gentle sunlight is warming my back as I make my way into the huge converted church that is home to my yoga class. The teacher, Dee, began running these classes a few years ago, not long after I started working at Harris & Erickson, and after seeing a leaflet stuck on a coffee shop notice board, I decided to give it a try to see if it helped with my stress levels. I can't say it did much for my stress overall, but I fell in love with the way yoga made me feel. How it made my body stronger and my mind sharper. I've been a devotee ever since and this class is a staple of my Saturday routine.

Yoga is also where I met Adelaide. At the time it seemed like serendipity. After a few classes where we ended up on mats next to each other, sharing our muttered moans of disbelief at some of the positions our goddess-like instructor could get herself into, we went out for a coffee one day. It was there that we discovered a mutual love of coffee and boy bands, as well as the fact that I was looking for a new assistant, while Addy had just completed her paralegal certification.

Kismet.

I find her as soon as I walk into the large room, in the back-right corner, our preferred spot. She's rolled out her mat and is sitting in a seated forward bend, stretching her hamstrings, which I know are sore from a session with her personal trainer a few days ago.

Things were awkward after our words yesterday and I know that was my fault, so sucking in a deep breath I walk over and greet her with a big smile. She eyes me cautiously, but it only takes a moment before a grin slides across her face.

"You're late, I wasn't sure if you were coming." There is no malice in her voice, only curiosity, and I'm grateful she's letting me off the hook and we can move on from yesterday.

I roll out my mat and take a spot on the ground beside her.

"Nanna called right before I was about to leave. Apparently she found a photo of us from a vacation we took to Saugatuck when I was ten, and it was imperative she tell me all about it right that instant." I can't help the giggle that slips past my lips when I remember how excited she sounded while she reminisced.

"You must miss them, how long has it been since they moved? Six months?"

"Yeah, almost that." I grimace as I stretch my own hamstrings, trying to loosen them up before class starts. The burn reminds me that I need to renew my gym membership. One yoga class a week just doesn't cut it. "They love Florida though, so that makes it easier. Every time I talk to them they sound happier than the last."

Adelaide pulls a bottle of water out of her bag and gulps some down, nodding in agreement. "That would definitely help. Still, how old were you when you started living with them? They're practically your parents. I couldn't imagine my parents not living here. Although, sometimes that sounds like a dream," she says wryly.

"I didn't live with them until I was sixteen. Mom left me with them a lot of the time, but I was always going back and forth between them and wherever she was living at the time." The familiar anxiety begins to creep up, remembering those years of tension and arguments. The confusion and dread that weighed me down daily. "When I was sixteen, I'd had enough of it all and I asked Nanna and Poppa if I could move in with them."

"Not gonna lie, your mom sounds like a legit nightmare."

I shrug and consider what she said. "She is who she is. I honestly don't think she wants to be this way, but at this point, I know she'll never change."

Our conversation comes to an end when Dee calls for everyone's attention, directing us to move into child's pose.

"Hey," Adelaide whispers. "Coffee after class?"

I pause, envisioning the pile of work on my desk and knowing I won't get into the office before lunchtime if I go with her.

"Of course," I whisper back.

CHAPTER TWO

MILES

I take a long swig of my beer and try to keep my eyes on the big-screen television that is playing the game above the bar. Despite my best efforts, they keep getting drawn to the table of girls to my left, where a cute blonde has been checking me out for the last ten minutes.

It has been almost a year since my disastrous television experience, which is an awkward amount of time. Too long for every sidelong glance to be a side effect of it, but too short to be able to discount that thought completely.

For all I know, blondie over there might just like what she sees. *Or* she's a rabid dilfie—DILF groupie— which is far more common than you would think, considering how much of an asshole that show portrayed me as.

B.L.—before Lulu—I would have been all over whatever she was offering. I was always on the hunt for *The One*. For my happily ever after. Always chasing what my parents had. After my daughter arrived, I realized I don't have the luxury of messing around with maybes and possibilities anymore.

It was what drew me to the whole shitshow that was *Dating the DILF* in the first place. What a stupid fucking name. I pick up the bottle and take another long pull of my beer, but the bitter rush of regret is all I taste.

A firm slap on my shoulder pulls my head out of my ass and I can't stop the grin when I look up and see my kid brother, Grayson, standing there.

"You have the same shitty expression that my last girlfriend had when I took her cat to the groomers and had them shave it to look like a lion." He pulls out the chair next to me and collapses into it. "She was so pissed, but it was funny as fuck and totally worth the week without sex."

"You're a dick." But I can't help but laugh when I imagine the look on his ex's face. She was a full-blown Kardashian wannabe with a huge stick up her ass and she treated that cat like a child.

The waitress comes over and we order a round of beers, my last for the night.

"Who's winning?" Gray nods toward the television.

"The Bulls are up by five, three minutes left until halftime."

We spend a few minutes catching up while we wait for our drinks to arrive and I have forgotten all about the girl from earlier when I feel a gentle tap on my shoulder and I turn around, only to come face to face with her.

"Hi." Her voice is low and kind of raspy, in an unexpected way. Incongruous to the girl-next-door vibe she gives off. "I'm so sorry to bother you, but my friends and I were talking and, well, are you the guy from that show?" She points to the table next to us. "My friends are convinced you're the guy from that DILF show."

Beside me, Gray covers his mouth to disguise a laugh while I have to swallow down the burn of impatience, the desperate desire to fuck right off and escape her predatory gaze.

But I have no one to blame but myself for this. I let myself get sweet-talked into something with bullshit promises when I should have known better.

So instead, I give her an appraising look and try to decide which camp she falls into. The women who approach me ultimately fall into one of two. The ones who want to rip my dick off and force-feed it to me or the women who want to do much more pleasurable things with it. Not that I would ever give them the chance.

She must mistake my silence for some kind of encouragement, because I feel a light tickle on my arm and, when I look down, I find her fingers trailing along it in a way that is a hell of a lot more intimate than it should be, considering I haven't spoken one word to her yet.

I guess that's my answer.

Remembering all the public relations lessons I got before the show, I slip on a mask of professionalism and give her a bland smile.

"That was me."

"Oh my God!" She squeals and turns to her friends. "It is him!" Turning back to me, she steps closer, her body now pressed up against my thigh. "You know, there's nothing hotter than a guy with a baby. You were so sweet with your little girl in that one episode."

Oh, fuck no.

"Yeah, that wasn't my daughter," I grit out. Making sure Lulu didn't appear on the show was the one *good* decision I made. But I know which episode she's talking about. It was a bogus babysitting setup with Toni? I think that's who it was anyway.

"Oh." She shrugs, her hand sliding lower until it's cupping my dick and she leans in, close enough to whisper suggestively. "Well, I really wanted to fuck you after that episode."

How to go from friendly stranger to inappropriate dilfie in one easy move, ladies and gentlemen.

"Whoa, okay, slow your roll there, beautiful," Grayson quickly interjects while I try to tamp down my annoyance. "I'm going to have to ask you to stop manhandling my brother and step away from the table."

The look on her face is pure shock and I can't help but chuckle as I remove her hand from my dick. "While I appreciate the offer, I'll have to pass."

I watch a myriad of emotions flit over her face before it settles on anger. "Whatever, you were an asshole anyway." And she does what could only be described as flounce back to her table.

"He really is," Gray calls out to her retreating back. "Consider yourself lucky you got away unscathed!"

She flips him the bird.

"I think I'm in love." He clutches his chest and blows her a kiss.

I laugh at his over-the-top theatrics, grateful he is here to diffuse the situation.

"Christ, I think that's the first time a girl's hand on my dick has ever made my balls shrivel up." I gulp down the rest of my beer.

"You're clearly not hanging around the right girls then." He grins over his drink.

"I don't even want to know what that means, fuckface."

"Shit, that reminds me." Gray puts his beer down and pulls his phone out of his pocket. "I saw this on my feed today and it's fucking hilarious. Hold, please." He starts scrolling, his finger is flying across the screen and he's already chuckling to himself. "Here."

He sticks his phone under my nose, and I see an old-fashion-style wanted poster with my face on it. Apparently, I'm wanted for being a "giant douche nozzle and most likely having a small penis." Reward is two hundred and fifty grand.

Huh, I would have thought I would be worth more than that.

I knock the phone out of his hand, and he curses at me as it lands on the table with a loud thud.

"What the fuck, man? That shit is expensive." He snatches it back up and cradles it to his chest while throwing me a wounded look.

Asshole.

"You know." He points at me, waving his finger

almost violently. "You used to have a much better sense of humor about this shit."

"Yeah, well, that was ten months, three million insults, two hundred and seventy-five thousand indecent proposals, one hundred and ninety thousand threats of violence, eighty-two marriage proposals, and twenty-three baby-momma offers ago." I lean back in my chair and shake my head. "Now it doesn't seem so funny."

He eyes me strangely. "That's oddly specific, but I take your point."

"I'm just sick of everyone thinking I'm a cheating little bitch."

"No one who knows you would ever believe that bullshit," he counters.

"It's not the people I know that I have to worry about." I know he's right. I know I shouldn't give a fuck what people think but I went on that goddamn show in the first place because I want to find love, and for a single dad running on fumes ninety percent of the time, the offer of having it hand delivered sounded too good to be true.

That should have told me something right there.

Now, every woman I meet thinks I'm either a complete scumbag, or a quick fuck to tell her friends about.

I scrub a hand across my face and sigh. "Ignore me, I'm just feeling pissy because Harvey has been harassing me about doing a reunion show."

"Seriously?" Gray's brows rise. "Didn't they just

finish a second series? How do they have time for reunion shows."

"I know, and there's another series starting next month too. Apparently the DILF is the gift that just keeps giving," I deadpan.

"Dating the DILF." He snickers. "Stupidest fucking name ever."

"Stupidest fucking *idea* ever."

We tap our bottles and cheers to that.

"I'm home." I throw my keys in the dish by the door, flinching as they hit the ceramic bowl and bring my fingers to my temple to massage gently. It's been a long day and my catch-up with Grayson wasn't nearly as relaxing as I had hoped it would be. All I want to do now is sit down in front of the television and relax.

The tiny footsteps that are flying toward me down the hall and the overexcited shrieking that accompanies them, are telling me that's not going to happen anytime soon.

"Daddyyyy!" A tiny blonde tornado throws herself into my arms and I thank whatever deity is watching over us that I have the foresight to brace myself for her onslaught.

"Hey, kiddo." I bend down and lift her up, inhaling her strawberry scent as she nuzzles into my neck. The stress of today falls away when her little arms tighten around my neck.

"Lulu, get your butt back here and finish your dinner," a gruff voice calls from down the hall.

A small growl vibrates against my neck and I try to contain a laugh. My daughter is not a fan of being told what to do.

"C'mon, what did Gramps make you tonight?"

"Nuggets." Her voice is barely a whisper and it seems that my enthusiastic welcome stole the last of her energy. I walk up the hall to our open-plan kitchen living area and her head rests on my shoulder, one hand gently rubbing her eye and the other wrapped around the back of my neck, twirling a lock of my hair around her finger. It's a quirk she's had since she was a baby and I think at this point I find it just as comforting as she does.

"Hey, Dad." I move through the galley-style kitchen and move straight to the dining table, gently placing Tallulah on her booster seat, not bothering with the straps.

She pushes her dinner plate away, a scowl marring her innocent face. "No. I'm done."

"Tallulah Renee, you've barely touched it. I want one more nugget, a spoonful of potatoes and a piece of broccoli eaten before you can be excused."

I duck my head to hide a grin and make my way to the refrigerator to grab a water. The only person I know who is more stubborn than my daughter is my father and seeing them clash is funny as fuck.

"Goddamn it, Gramps!"

Until it isn't.

Turning, I glare at my dad who is rubbing a hand

over his jaw, his brow furrowed, before I shift toward Tallulah.

"That little outburst has cost you your television time tonight. Now eat your dinner." I narrow my eyes at her, and my strict father act must do the trick because she starts shoveling food in her mouth without arguing.

"Jesus Christ, Dad," I hiss when I'm far enough away that Tallulah won't hear me. "You've got to be more careful around her. I swear to God, I heard her say fuck the other day. Then she just stared at me with this angelic look on her face. You're turning my daughter into a deviant."

Dad folds his arms across his chest and looks me hard in the eye. "You're never going to stop her from hearing the words, Miles. It's up to you to teach her not to repeat them."

I huff out a laugh. "That's easier said than done, Old Man."

He pierces me with a glare, and I decide not to push my luck and change the subject.

"She looks exhausted, what did you guys get up to today?" I round the island bench and take a seat, keeping Tallulah within my sights.

"That kid from number seven came over for a play-date." He groans painfully. "Talk about a deviant, *that* kid has a court date in his future, mark my words. Here." My stomach growls loudly at the sight of the plate of food he slides in front of me. "You look tired too. Bad day?"

I chew my food, happy to have some time to

consider my answer, knowing that Dad will have little to no sympathy for my situation.

"Harvey got a hold of my new number and was calling all day." My throat tightens remembering his smarmy voice and the new promises he was throwing around.

"You were a damn idiot getting involved in all of those shenanigans in the first place. I warned you." He shakes his head, disappointment pulsing off him. "Thomas and I both warned you."

He's got me there. He and my big brother did warn me, and when my life came crashing down ten months ago, they were the first to say I told you so. But they were also the first to step in and help me get control back, which takes the sting away from the continued barbs they throw my way.

"I know, Dad." I imagine my face is as petulant as my almost-three-year-old's was ten minutes ago and I try to school my features into a less hostile version of myself.

"Daddy, I'm tired."

I turn to see Tallulah almost falling asleep at the table. I sigh and push away from the island bench where I was eating.

"I'm going to give Lulu her bath, you're good to let yourself out?"

"Yeah." He begins gathering up the dirty dishes and rinsing them. "Go, I'll see you tomorrow morning."

I move to walk behind him and slap him on the back. "Thanks, Dad. I really do appreciate all your help."

He meets my eye, understanding clear and bright. "I know," he answers brusquely. His eyes turn to his granddaughter and his heavy expression suddenly lightens, a grin spreading across his face. "I think you're needed."

I follow the direction of his look and see Tallulah, fast asleep in her mashed potatoes.

CHAPTER THREE

CHARLOTTE

Adelaide: I swear Thompson has a butt plug permanently shoved up his ass.

Adelaide: I mean have you seen the way he walks?

Adelaide: Like a goddamn penguin!

Adelaide: It's unnatural, Charlie. UNNATURAL!

A tired, but good-natured sigh slips past my lips as I read Addy's response to my earlier message. Pulling my keys out of the ignition, I sink back into my seat and type a quick reply.

Charlie: That may be so, but I believe my question was: did you file the paperwork for his continuance?

Adelaide: Yes, I understand that was your question, but I believe it was pertinent that I shared my

observation before I forgot. Because it was funny as fuck, *Charlotte*

Adelaide: And, yes, I filed the paperwork. <rolls eyes>

Groaning, I shove my phone in my purse and take a moment to shake off the stress of the week.

Ice cream. I need ice cream. A pint of mint choc chip will make everything better. It's the one golden rule of life that has proven to be true over and over.

Ice cream fixes everything.

I climb out of my beloved Prius, ignoring the bite of my waistband and instead concentrate on the mission at hand. My determination is admirable, if I do say so myself.

A light mist of rain has begun to fall, so I hurry through the parking lot to the beckoning fluorescent lights of the supermarket, the familiar tap of my heels on the asphalt comforting me.

Rushing through the automatic sliding doors, I make a sharp right turn and head straight to the freezer section. This week has been a complete nightmare and all I want to do right now is head home and climb into bed with my delicious, sugary treats and a smart-ass devil called *Lucifer*.

Right on cue, I notice how my pants are stretching uncomfortably across my ass with every step I take, reminding me how long it has been since I spent any time on the treadmill. That would probably be a much better plan.

However, all thoughts of the treadmill disappear when I reach the ice cream section and I stare at the promised land. My eyes dart across the rows of creamy goodness looking for my beloved mint choc chip and the noise that escapes my lips when I can't see it could almost be described as a growl.

A deep chuckle to my right grabs my attention and my cheeks are already flaming before I even turn to see who was witness to my small display of emotion.

The burn intensifies when I find myself face to face with one of the most gorgeous men I have ever seen. The first thing I notice is his height. He towers over me, and considering I stand at five foot seven in bare feet, that almost never happens.

Vibrant blue eyes meet mine, full of mischief, and I allow myself a moment to imagine what it would feel like to look into eyes like that every day. The thought startles me and the moment comes to a quick end when he clears his throat and his teeth sink into his full bottom lip in, what I can only assume is, an attempt to fight the smile quirking his full lips.

A fight he is losing.

A wave of fresh embarrassment washes over me and I duck my head in an effort to avoid his gaze.

"Don't you just hate it when they don't have your favorite flavor?" I force a smile and turn to move away, desperate to leave this moment of disappointment and mortification behind, when the deep timbre of his voice stops me.

"Trust me, nobody feels more passionately about ice cream than I do."

I glance up and take in his easy expression. He's running a hand through his slightly unkempt, dark blond hair, a grin stretching across his face. I notice that his hair isn't artfully tousled. You know the kind of messy that guys spend far too long on, in an effort to make it look effortless? Instead, it looks as though he spends his days running his hand through it, with zero care for his appearance. I try not to question why that endears this stranger to me.

"If they don't have my *Cherry Garcia,* I will burn this place to the ground." He leans toward me conspiratorially. "Can I trust you to have my back if shit goes down?"

My answering laugh is loud and unexpected. Somehow this guy has managed to put me at ease and soothe my awkwardness.

"Of course. Who better to have by your side at a time like that than a fellow ice cream annihilator, stranger or not," I reply, my face the picture of earnestness.

"See, now, you get it!" He shakes his head gravely. "Not many people do."

"Well, fortunately there is plenty of *Cherry Garcia* for you." I nod toward a row full—*full!*—of his addiction. "So it looks like Whole Foods will live to see another day. But unless they get in more mint choc chip pretty damn quick, I can't guarantee how long that will stay true."

His smile matches mine and I try to remember when I have felt such an instant connection to a guy before. Have I ever? If I was a different person, I would flirt a little, and maybe ask him out for a drink. That's what a normal twenty-nine-year-old would do on a Friday night, right?

"I'm Miles, by the way." He offers me a large hand. "I figure if we're plotting to take down grocery stores together, we should probably be on a first-name basis."

I stare blankly at his hand for a moment, trying to remember the last time someone shook my hand in any setting other than business. Failing to find one, I slip my much smaller hand into his and smile at the warmth that immediately fills me.

"Charlotte." We stand there, probably looking like idiots, slowly shaking hands, our eyes glued to each other and I am pretty damn sure the dopey smile he is wearing is mirrored on my own face.

That's when it hits me. We're having a moment. A *moment*, moment. Like in my romance novels when the guy and girl meet and BAM! Instant connection that inevitably leads to a happily ever after.

I'm having a goddamn real-life meet cute. Who knew those things ever actually happened? Not me, that's for freaking sure.

His eyes, that have been slowly moving over my face like a gentle caress (because, yes, this moment is *that* swoony), suddenly zero in on something over my shoulder and widen with delighted excitement.

"It looks like today is both of our lucky day." He points behind me, and when I realize what he is showing me, my grin widens. A lone pint of my adored ice cream has been pushed haphazardly in amongst a row of *Strawberry Cheesecake*. As I stare at the tub, I have to fight the urge to show Miles my gratitude with my tongue. Because if I lick it, it's mine, right?

Shaking my head to dislodge the image, a satisfied sigh slips out on an exhale. Ice cream and a hot guy all in one night? Maybe it is my lucky day.

"I could kiss you right now." Turning, I bend down to grab the ice cream, trying to ignore the pounding of my heart that began the instant his eyes heated at my declaration.

Unfortunately, that's when it happens. The unmistakable sound of fabric tearing. I freeze, the moment suspended in time, as I realize the snug fit of my pants across my ass is now feeling pretty damn comfortable.

And breezy. Definitely breezy.

I'm frozen in horror, my eyes squeezed tightly shut, when the humiliation seeps in and I fully grasp the fact that my thong-clad ass is now on full display for Miles to enjoy.

I guess it's safe to say our moment is well and truly over.

"What did you do?" Adelaide screeches at me, her face a picture of horrified glee.

"I dropped the ice cream and ran out of there as fast as I could with my purse covering my ass." My face is on fire and I am just as embarrassed now, recounting the story, as I was on Friday night. "If I'm ever tempted to let my gym membership lapse again, or I forget to take my dry cleaning in and am forced to wear pants that haven't fit since I was a college senior, you have permission to remind me of this horror."

Adelaide smirks at me and I can already see her formulating some smart-ass reply, so I cut her off before she can make me feel any worse.

"I know, I know. You'll be happy to send me a continuous stream of memes that will succeed in never letting me forget the moment or live it down."

Her eyes widen innocently. "It's what any *real* friend would do, Charlie."

"Get out!"

She snorts out an unattractive laugh and makes her way out of my office before pausing at the entrance.

"Charlie?" she starts, in a very un-Adelaide-like way. I hesitate for a moment, but then give her the nod to continue.

"I really am sorry it ended like that, but I've got to say, it's kind of nice to see you finally being affected by someone like that." She shakes her head, a look of concern settling over her face. "I mean, for a while there I was really beginning to worry that you might be an emotionless robot sent from the future to destroy all of mankind." She scrunches her nose. "It's good to know you're simply an introvert who hates people. I feel like I can relax now."

"Get out!"

She pokes her tongue out at me and finally leaves, pulling the door closed behind her.

I groan loudly and bang my head down onto my desk. Adelaide has a point though, I have to give her that. It's also not the first time someone has insinuated that I'm too unemotional. My childhood was what could politely be called chaotic. Growing up with a mother who didn't really care for the job too much, preferring to spend her time gambling and looking for the next man to support her, I always felt as though I was in a never-ending state of flux. If it wasn't for my grandparents, I wouldn't have had any kind of stability at all.

After a childhood like that, I crave balance and emotional consistency. Both of which are nearly impossible to find in personal relationships and I realized early on that I was much happier when left to myself. With the exception of my childhood best friend, Wyatt, Adelaide is my only real friend. Considering she's my assistant, most people would find that sad. I find it a relief.

But my encounter with Miles has definitely left me rattled. I enjoyed bantering with him. Bantering? When did I become a woman who banters? I have to admit, if only to myself, that I felt more alive in that five-minute exchange than I possibly ever have before. While I would expect the strength of that emotion, and the vulnerability it opens me up to, to terrify me, all I'm craving is the need for more.

And I think that is what frightens me most of all.

Sitting up, I rub the heel of my hand across my chest in an attempt to dislodge the tightness there. It is all a moot point anyway. The odds I'll ever run into Miles again are probably a million to one.

I had my chance and I blew it, but I make a promise

to myself that if I ever do see him again, I will put my big girl panties on, and I'll ask him out.

Of course, I make this promise knowing full well it will never happen. I can't decide if that is karma being cruel or kind, but either way, I'm confident I won't be seeing Miles again.

CHAPTER FOUR

"Scruffy is going to be fine, Mrs. Connelly. Get this medication into him twice a day and he'll be chasing Frida's cat again before you know it."

"Thank you, Miles." She looks at me and the deep-set wrinkles around her eyes sharpen as she smiles at me kindly. "I was so worried."

She lifts the tiny dog into her arms and a tiny grunt slips out at the effort. I can't help but wish she would be as vigilant with her own health as she is with her pet.

I take her by the elbow and lead her out to the front office where our receptionist will take care of the bill.

"Kyla, it was level five consult today for Mrs. Connelly." Her eyes soften in understanding and she nods before turning to the computer to work her magic.

I lean down to the elderly woman in front of me and give her hand a gentle squeeze.

"If Scruffy isn't looking better in a day or two, don't

hesitate to call me, okay? You have my cell number, so I can be reached at any time."

She nuzzles into the small dog, peppering his head with kisses. "Thank you, Miles. I appreciate that, I really do."

Turning, I stride to my office and glance at my watch. Fifteen minutes until my next appointment. Determined to get to my computer so I can continue my Facebook search for every Charlotte that lives in Chicago, I quicken my steps.

Settling at my desk, I have just pulled up my social media when my door bursts open.

"Another 'level five' consult? You're going to put us out of business." Camden, my business partner and best friend, glares at me across the room. "That medication you gave her was worth a couple hundred dollars alone, Miles. I've got kids to feed, you know." He sighs in exasperation.

I smirk at him, knowing how much it will infuriate him. A level five consult is a code I came up with to let Kyla know she is only to bill the patient a flat fifty-dollar fee.

"Jesus, relax, Cam. I cover the rest of the bill out of my own pocket. Tyson and Brianna's Happy Meals are safe, I swear." Shaking my head, I try to subtly turn the computer screen so he can't see it, without him noticing. "How'd you find out anyway?"

"I heard you mention it to Kyla a couple of weeks ago and she told me. I meant to bring it up then, but I got distracted." He stalks across my office and plants his ass on the corner of my desk. "Your heart is bigger than your bank balance, dude. Has been ever since college. I hope you know when you go bankrupt, you're not sleeping on my couch."

"I would expect nothing less, you asshole. Now, did you want something else or are you just here to bust my balls. I have a patient in"—I grab my phone and check the time—"nine minutes."

"Just here to bust your— What's that?" He raises an eyebrow at me and nods toward the screen in front of me.

"It's a computer, genius. Are you sure you graduated college?" I try my best to deflect, but I already know he won't let this go.

"That, my friend, is Facebook. You haven't been on Facebook since—"

"Yeah, I know," I cut him off. "I just figured enough time had passed and I wanted to catch up on things."

"I don't know, man." He rolls his shoulders as though trying to release the tension that is suddenly vibrating through the room. "I still see some pretty fucking epic memes about you doing the rounds. It hasn't been that long. Wait." He peers at the screen. "Who is Charlotte Chicago?"

I quickly minimize the screen, which is what I should have done as soon as Camden walked in. Clearly, I'm no brainiac, either.

"No one." I push away from my desk and start to stand, only for Cam to push me back down to sit.

"*Not* no one." His eyes narrow shrewdly. "Did you meet someone?"

My mind flashes briefly to the gorgeous brunette

from Whole Foods. I haven't felt that way talking to a woman in a long time. Like I was myself again. Not the defensive, waiting-for-shit-to-hit-the-fan guy I've been for the last ten months. She was beautiful, there is no doubt about that. But it was the intelligence in her bright green eyes and the way her smile lit up her entire face that really captivated me. That one smile brightened her whole aesthetic and she went from unapproachable beauty to a girl I can imagine watching sappy romantic comedies with while cuddling on the sofa.

Not that I'm into rom-coms or cuddling. I'm clearly far too masculine for that.

I give a reluctant sigh because I have known Camden long enough to know he won't let this drop.

"I might have met someone," I begrudgingly admit. "But we were—" I pause and consider how to continue, Charlotte's face bright with embarrassment clear in my mind. I doubt that's a story she would want me to spread around. "Interrupted and I didn't have a chance to get her number."

"So, you're Facebook stalking her with just a first name and city?" He snorts at me in amusement. "Well, good luck with that."

"Yeah, it's not looking good," I admit wryly.

Camden stands and stretches his long arms over his head, groaning. "Before I forget, Shannon wants to invite you guys to dinner tomorrow night, are you free?"

"I'm always available for Shannon. Feel free to make yourself scarce though, it's been too long since I had some alone time with your wife." I waggle my eyebrows at him, highly enjoying the annoyance that flits over his face.

"Stop trying to hit on my wife, asshole. Besides, the kids will all be there so there will be no alone time."

"Ah, well, that sucks."

"Welcome to my life, dick." He starts to leave before he stops and turns back. "I really do hope you find her." He nods back to the computer. "Your girl. I know how hard it's been since— Well, I know you've had a tough time these last few years, and people have said a lot of shit about you, but you're a good guy and you deserve to be happy." He kneads his neck, obviously uncomfortable with this heart-to-heart. "Even if you do like my wife a little *too* much."

I watch him leave, laughing, and then turn back to my computer.

Charlotte Chicago, where are you?

"Daddy?" Lulu snuggles down into her blankets as I close the pages of *Love You Forever* and lie down next to her, placing a kiss on her forehead.

"What's up, kiddo?"

"It's my birthday 'morrow?"

I chuckle quietly at the question she has asked every day since we went to Tyson's birthday party last weekend.

I stretch my arms up and place them behind my head. "Not even close, kid. It's still a few months away."

I turn to look at her and see her bottom lip is sticking out in a goddamn pout.

I'm so screwed when she's a teenager.

"How about we go to the aquarium tomorrow? We haven't gone to see the penguins in a long time." I cross my fingers that her penguin obsession will be enough to distract her from her birthday delusions.

She rolls over and curls into me, her hand reaching up to play with my hair. "No, we go see Momma."

My eyes immediately search out the picture on her dresser. It was taken on Renee's twenty-first birthday and she looks young, beautiful, and happy. It's how I will always remember her.

"You want to go visit Momma?"

"Yup. We gonna eat cake." Lulu giggles against my chest, the sound easing the tension that was beginning to pulse in my temple.

Losing Renee was the worst moment of my life wrapped up in the very best moment. An undiagnosed heart condition resulted in her having a fatal heart attack during Lulu's birth. In one horrifying moment, I lost my best friend and gained a tiny human who was dependent on me for everything, and there are times I still don't know how I made it through those early days.

We talk about her mother often. I've always been determined to somehow keep the memory of her alive for Lulu, which sometimes feels impossible. How do you help your daughter bond with a picture? Or a story? How do I make her *feel* the love her mother had for her, when she never got a chance to experience it?

So, I do the best I can. I tell her every story I have of the two of us. I tell her every detail I can remember about her mom, no matter how small. I make sure she knows that Renee's love of waterfalls inspired her name, but that it didn't come close to the love she had for Lulu. On Renee's birthday and every Mother's Day, we head to the cemetery where we leave a card and eat cupcakes, so she has a tangible place to connect with her mom.

And every day I hope like fuck it's enough.

"You're right, we should go visit her." I've tried to limit her time at the cemetery because, to be honest, I worry it's too morbid when she's so young. But maybe it's time to rethink that. "How about we stop by the bakery and get Mom's favorite cupcakes and then we'll visit with her. Sound like a plan?"

"'S a good plan." She sighs and minutes later I'm listening to her tiny rumbling snores and sending up a prayer to Renee that I don't completely mess this parenting shit up.

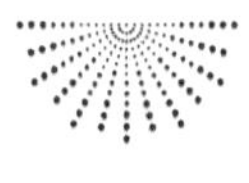

CHARLOTTE

"Wait, wait, wait, wait, wait, wait, *wait*," I hiss. The sound of my phone is momentarily overtaken by the thud of metal against drywall as I shoulder my way through the door. Kicking it shut behind me, I try to ignore the sting in my fingers while I juggle a pile of files, desperately trying to keep them from all falling to the ground.

I make it to the console table in my entrance and dump them down, watching them slide along the smooth wooden surface. My gym bag slips to my elbow, wrenching my shoulder, and I grimace at the burn.

Aware that my phone is about to slide over to voicemail and I don't want to miss this call, I answer without checking the caller ID.

I really should know better.

"Hello, Charlotte Reed speaking."

"Baby girl, you sound so professional!" My mother's

shrill voice greets me. "When did you get so grown up?"

I pull the phone away from my ear and double-check the screen. Yep, definitely *not* the call I was expecting about the lawsuit I am currently working my ass off to settle.

"Hi, Mom, how are you?" I ask reluctantly, already knowing I don't have time for whatever self-inflicted drama is causing havoc in her life right now.

"Good, baby, I'm good. I spoke to your grandparents today," she starts, her voice suspiciously happy. "They seem to be loving it in Florida."

"They are," I confirm, my hackles well and truly raised.

"Grandma mentioned that you snagged a huge client for the firm. I'm so proud of you, Charlie."

Tension tightens my shoulders and, despite the pride I feel about bringing Preston Pharmaceuticals into the fold at Harris & Erickson, I have very little desire to discuss this with my mother.

"I did." My response is curt, maybe even rude, but I *know* my mother. She uses my happiness against me, taking each moment of my joy and manipulating it to get what she wants. As though every one of my good moods or victories is a free pass for her to demand something from me.

"So, listen, I'm a little short on rent this month and I was wondering if I could borrow a few hundred dollars to tide me over until I get paid."

And there it is.

"I gave you money a couple of months ago, Mom. I can't afford to keep doing this all the time."

"This is the last time, baby, I swear. It's just been a rough month, a lot of unexpected bills, but I promise this is it." She's doing her best to sound sincere, but it's forced and there is a hint of desperation that hangs heavy in the air.

My throat constricts as I listen to her promise. *This is the last time, baby, I swear.* It's the same promise I've been listening to since I got my first job at fourteen, and I'm so tired of it. So fucking tired of being disappointed and let down.

Too tired to fight it anymore.

My eyes roam over the wall in front of me, staring unseeingly at the hideous floral wallpaper I want to get rid of, and my fingers play with the hem of my jacket. I'm about to agree, to tell her I'll send the money through, but my mother always was impatient, and she takes my moment of silence as a refusal.

"You owe me, Charlotte." All warmth has evaporated from her voice and all that is left is recrimination. "All that money you cost me while you were growing up. Clothes and food and everything else you wanted that I couldn't afford. I made sure you had it all, the least you can do is help me out now." Her voice drops slightly, as though she has moved the phone away from her mouth. "You always were a selfish little bitch."

The words pierce my chest before they penetrate my conscious thought, but as soon as they do, the familiar burn behind my eyes kicks in.

"Bye, Mom." I hang up the phone and take a few deep, steadying breaths before I pull up my banking app and transfer her the money.

My legs are aching, and I am almost running to try and keep up with my mom. It's only a short walk from the bus stop to Grandma and Grandpa's place but I'm so tired and it's so hot. I can feel the sweat dripping down my back into my butt and it's so, so gross.

I had such a good time at the carnival today, though. I ate so much bad food and went on all the rides. I didn't think Mommy was going to let me go on the roller coaster, but she said I was big enough now. It was so much fun!

"Mom, wait up." I run to catch up with her, but she keeps going, not slowing down at all.

"Hurry up, Charlotte, your grandma is expecting us for dinner."

Mom sounds grumpy, but she has been ever since we got on the bus. My face feels warm when I remember what she looked like as she searched her purse for change for our fares. Everybody was looking at us and I didn't like it.

"Mom, I'm tired." I stop for a moment to catch my breath. My legs are little, and I can't keep up with her.

"Charlotte." She finally stops and turns to look at me, but when she does it just makes me scared. She looks angry, so I do the only thing I can and let a scowl settle on my face, so she doesn't see how scared I am of her.

She walks up to me, angrily snatching my hand and pulling me to walk alongside her.

"Walk, Charlotte. Now." We take a few steps and then she looks down at me, catching my eye. "We've had such a nice day, why do you have to ruin it?" She shakes her head and looks away. "Why do you always ruin everything?"

The crisp white wine slides down my throat, the almost imperceptible sweetness stimulating my taste buds, and I have to stop myself from gulping down the entire glass.

Sliding my glass onto the coffee table, I groan when I notice the ring of condensation left by the cold glass. I really should be using a wine glass like a grown-up, not a tumbler. But then I also should probably be drinking wine from a bottle, not a box, so what are you going to do? Curling up on the sofa, I drag my eyes back to the document on my tablet, trying to concentrate, but it doesn't take long before I realize that I have no hope of accomplishing anything tonight. Mom's phone call has left me too distracted.

Shutting my tablet down and gathering up the files I brought home, I move to the front foyer and place it all by the front door, promising myself I'll go into the office early tomorrow to make up for it.

I'm about to head upstairs for a long hot shower, followed by Netflix to lull me to a hopefully dreamless —although if the past month is any indication, the mysterious Miles will no doubt appear—sleep, when a noise catches my attention. Pausing by the stairs, one hand already holding on to the banister, I take a moment to listen and it's not long before I hear it again. A soft mewl that seems to be coming from my front porch.

Opening the door, I turn on the porch light and I immediately spot what is making the pitiful sound. A tiny gray kitten is curled up on the top step, shivering despite the warm air.

A tightening in my chest has me moving forward.

"Hey, boy. Come here, sweet boy." I make some kissy noises and I probably look completely ridiculous to anyone walking past right now, as I try to keep my movements as nonthreatening as possible so as not to scare the cat away.

I needn't worry though. The kitten looks at me with the saddest eyes and doesn't move. When I reach the tiny creature, I kneel down and scoop him up, softly cooing, and pull him to my chest.

Now that I have my hands on him, I can see exactly how small he is, and I realize he can't be more than a few weeks old. I look for a collar with a tag but find nothing. It's then that I notice he has a deep cut at the tip of one of his ears and the fur around it is matted with blood.

"Oh, sweet boy, c'mon, I've got you." I walk back inside, grabbing up my phone off the console table and google the nearest vet.

McConnell Street Veterinary Clinic. I glance at the time and see that I only have thirty minutes until it closes, and so I quickly run upstairs and grab a blanket to wrap the kitten up in. Then, making sure I have my purse and phone, I settle him in the front passenger seat of my car.

I'm not even sure if this clinic takes walk-in appointments, but what sort of vet would turn away an injured pussy?

Ten minutes later, I am pulling into the parking lot of the large clinic, one hand on the steering wheel and the other softly petting the kitten, listening to his contented mewls.

The clinic is still brightly lit, and I can see people moving around inside which sends a flood of relief through me. Gathering the fluffy bundle in my arms, I make my way inside and head straight for the reception desk.

A petite redhead with kind eyes and a name tag that reads *KYLA*, greets me warmly. "Good evening, how can I help you tonight?"

"Hi, I'm sorry I don't have an appointment," I start, apologetically. "But I found this little guy on my porch a little while ago and he has a pretty nasty cut on his ear. I know you're closing soon but I was wondering if the vet could take a look at him?"

Her brows furrow and concern is written all over her face. She leans over the desk, peering at his little face. "Of course, he can, follow me."

Kyla walks us over to a small examination room that is empty and motions for me to go in.

"Take a seat. Dr. Kent is with a patient at the moment, but I'll send him in as soon as he's finished. It shouldn't be too long." She smiles warmly at me and hands me a clipboard with some forms. "If you wouldn't mind completing these while you're waiting, I can get you in our system."

"Of course." I gently lay the kitten on the chair beside me, place my purse under it and, using the pen attached to the clipboard, I begin filling the forms out.

I have just finished writing down my phone number when the door opens.

"Hi, I'm Dr. Kent. I hear you found a—" I turn to face the vet, curious why he cut himself off, and come face to face with the last person I ever expected to see.

Miles.

Cherry Garcia Miles.

I want to run. Maybe perform an Olympic-worthy sprint out of this room, that suddenly feels far too small to contain the both of us. With the adrenaline running through me right now, I'm pretty sure I could be at my car before he even realizes what is happening. I mean, there is always the chance I might fall flat on my face like when I agreed to go running with Adelaide but, really, what are the odds of that happening *three* times?

A soft meow distracts me from my escape plans and my fingers slide through the kitten's soft fur while my eyes dart around the impersonal examination room, looking everywhere except at the man in front of me. Until his amused voice gives me no choice.

"Charlotte Chicago. You are a hard lady to find."

CHAPTER SIX

MILES

*W*ell, fuck me.

It's been about a month since our encounter at the grocery store. And by *"about* a month" I mean four weeks, four days, and roughly two hours.

I gave up on my random internet searches after a week because, let's face it, the odds of me ever finding her were pretty much zilch. I guess the universe had other ideas and I make a mental note to pay this amazing karma forward as soon as possible.

I step back and take a moment to observe her. Just as I did at the supermarket, I search her face for any hint of recognition but once again, I see none. Her face is flushed, and she refuses to meet my eye. Her fingertips, which are painted a pale pink color—when the hell did I start noticing women's nail polish?—are furiously sliding through the coat of the kitten on the chair beside her. All in all, she looks thoroughly embarrassed and altogether perfect.

When my dick starts to take a little too much notice

of the way her mouth is shaped into a perfect O, I clear my throat and attempt to act like the professional I'm supposed to be.

"You found a stray cat?" I do my very best to keep my voice level and ignore the charged atmosphere in the room. It seems to do the trick because her head snaps up and she looks at me with eyes full of worry.

"I did, he was on my porch and he has a cut on his ear." She pulls the tiny kitten onto her lap and gently points to the matted fur on its ear. "It looks pretty nasty."

I take a couple of steps forward and ignoring my baser instincts, the ones that have me wanting to touch every inch of exposed skin I can find, I kneel down and examine the cat closely.

Our foreheads are so close as we both lean over the tiny furball and, for a moment, I imagine lifting my head up and letting my mouth taste her. I wonder how her lips would feel. If they would be soft and yielding or would they fight me? Taunting and eager to take what they can from me.

Then her pussy mewls pitifully, and I realize that I am undeniably an asshole.

I clear my throat once again and, lifting my arms slightly, I quirk a questioning brow at her. "May I?"

She understands and passes the cat over to me. I ignore the jolt of electricity that seems to follow her touch and move over to the examination table.

"Yeah, that definitely doesn't look good." She has followed me to the table and her eyes are closely watching every move I make, which I'm finding pretty damn distracting. "I'll clean the wound and it will need a couple of stitches. Normally, I'd scan her for a microchip, but she can't be more than a few weeks old, so she's too young to have had the procedure."

Charlotte is nodding along, listening closely.

"I can call the local animal shelter if you want me to? They'll come out and pick her up within the hour."

"Oh." She appears startled by my suggestion and when her small hand finds its way to the even tinier paw and begins to rub it comfortingly, I know she has already lost her heart to the pocket-sized kitten.

"I'm happy to keep him. I don't want him to go to a shelter."

Her hands are once again smoothing through the cat's gray coat. "Her," I murmur distractedly.

"What?" Charlotte responds, looking confused.

"Uh, her." I shake my head, making a concerted effort to pull my head out of my ass. "The cat's a girl."

"Oh. *Her.* I'm happy to keep her."

"Okay, I don't see why you shouldn't. She has no collar, so there's no way of locating an owner." I step away and wash my hands at the small sink in the corner of the office. "Perhaps you could give me your phone number?" Her surprised expression clashes with my own, which is a picture of calm. I am not going to fuck this up.

"Just in case anyone comes in looking for a lost pet," I reassure her. "I doubt it will happen, but I'd hate for you to get caught up in convoluted catnapping charges. I mean, you get thrown in the slammer and you'd have to give up life's little luxuries like bad romantic comedies, strawberry milkshakes and—" I pause for a moment, making sure I have her attention before I continue. "Mint choc chip ice cream."

I offer her a small smile and watch with a certain amount of enjoyment as her face turns beet red and her shoulders slump slightly.

She seems to be so put together, the type of woman who is always in control and this small display of emotion feels like it's completely out of character for her. I like that I affect her this way and I have to tamp down the desire to tease her a little more, just to see how she would react.

"Oh God." She groans, sending a jolt straight to my dick. "Can we please forget that ever happened? I don't think I've ever been so embarrassed in my life."

"You don't have anything to be embarrassed about," I say this over my shoulder as I start preparing the instruments I'll need for the sutures.

"You saw my ass." She sounds cautiously amused.

I turn and I can't help my smirk. "It's a great ass." I shrug before continuing. "Let me just go and grab my nurse and we'll get these stitches taken care of."

She nods, and when I step out into the now empty waiting room, I discreetly adjust myself and then go in search of Kyla.

Twenty minutes later we have said goodbye to Kyla and the cat is falling asleep in Charlotte's arms, thanks to the painkillers I gave her, and I'm going over some instructions with Charlotte.

"She'll be fine, so long as the wound stays clean. Just

try and keep her inside for a few days and bring her back next week so I can see how she's doing."

"I will, thank you."

She's been much more relaxed since I broke the ice and mentioned *Ass-gate*, as I've come to think of it, so I decide to press my luck.

"Look, Charlotte—"

"Charlie," she cuts me off. "My friends call me Charlie."

"Charlie." I smile and I know I probably look like a complete dick right now, so I take a moment to appreciate the fact that Camden isn't here to witness my first step toward pussy-whipped-ness. "I'm just going to lay it all out there. I think you're beautiful and funny and I'd like to take you out for a drink and get to know you more."

It takes a moment for her to respond, and when she does, it's not what I was hoping for.

"You saw my ass." Her voice is barely above a whisper and she's biting her lip anxiously.

"I did," I agree. "Would it help if I show you my ass?" Her eyes widen and then drop down to my butt as though trying to see through my jeans. "I mean, my ass is nowhere near as spectacular as yours, but if it'll make you feel better about seeing me again, I'll drop trou right here."

Her laugh is light and genuine, and she looks almost surprised, as though the sound is foreign to her. Right then and there I decide I want to hear it again. And again. And possibly a-fucking-gain.

"That won't be necessary." The heat in her eyes tells

me that's not the answer she *wants* to give me. "Okay, one drink can't hurt, right?"

"One, five, let's just see how the night plays out?"

She giggles, fucking *giggles,* and suddenly my dick is standing to attention as though he thinks that sound deserves a standing ovation. I shift uncomfortably, grateful for the clipboard in my hand.

"My number is on the form I gave to your nurse, message me and we can arrange something."

Before I can come up with a witty reply, she's walking out the door, kitten bundled in her arms, and an unmistakable sway to her hips.

"Pass the corn, Nugget."

Tallulah eyes Grayson like he just asked her to kill a puppy and pulls the bowl of corn toward her chest.

"No."

Gray looks at her plate which is remarkably free of any corn since she can't stand it. "You don't even like it," he returns indignantly.

"Do to."

"No, you don't."

"Do."

"Don't."

"For Christ's sake, Grayson," my dad barks.

"Christ's sake, Ryson."

"Tallulah, no," I warn. "Dad, seriously?"

"Yeah, Gramps, seriously?" Gray pokes his tongue

out at a giggling Lulu. "Could you at least *try* to be a good example for Nugget?"

I shake my head and look around the table. It's Friday night which in the Kents' world is family night. Tonight, we're at my brother Thomas' house, which somehow manages to be immaculate despite the fact that three kids under the age of seven live here, and both Tom and his wife, Chrissy, work full-time jobs. They're the type of people who give you a complex about how bad you're fucking up life in comparison to them, but they're so nice you can't hate them for it.

It's completely aggravating.

My nieces and nephew, Tully, Carson, and Shae, are laughing right along with Lulu at Grayson's antics as he continues to goad my dad. Thomas is watching with an amused smile and Chrissy is fussing over the kids' plates, trying to encourage them to eat more. All in all, an average Friday night and undeniably my happy place.

Despite our no-cell phone rule, I slide mine out of my pocket and try to check it on the sly. Charlie and I have messaged a few times over the last couple of days. Not a lot, but it's been enough to keep me on my toes anticipating our next exchange.

"Expecting a call?"

I look up to see Tom watching me with a quirked eyebrow.

"No, not a call." I look to make sure Lulu is distracted and paying me no attention before I continue. "I met someone." The grin that spreads across my face is met with a look of concern and a hint of suspicion.

"You met someone? Where?"

"At the grocery store." I take a bite of roast chicken and chew while Tom considers what I've said.

"You just met some random girl in a supermarket and asked her out? Do you really think that's the best idea? What if she saw you on the show and is looking for a story to sell to the tabloids?"

It's times like this I feel sorry for my big brother. Always the responsible one, it's as though he can never just experience the joy of a moment. He's always considering and calculating. Worrying about some nameless disaster that only he can see coming.

"I don't think she has a clue who I am," I tell him honestly. "She took off before I could even get a number, but then she came into the clinic with a stray cat on Tuesday. It was fate." I smirk at him, knowing how much that will rile him up. Thomas Kent is far too practical to believe in fate.

"You've been watching too many Sandra Bullock movies," he says with a smile, which is quickly replaced with a look of unease. "That's pretty damn coincidental. She just happened to stroll into your clinic? I mean the fact that you work there is pretty well known. It wouldn't take much for her to find out."

I try to bite down my annoyance at his pessimism. He can't help his overly cautious nature any more than Grayson can control his need for the last word. I glance around the table to make sure everyone is still preoccupied before giving Tom a hard look.

"That's not what this is, and even if it is, it's my mistake to make."

"Jesus, Miles, don't you think you've made enough mistakes to last a lifetime?" Tom's voice is tight with tension. "First a one-night stand that changed your life forever and then a goddamn ridiculous reality show. Maybe, if you stopped acting like mistakes are a badge of honor, you'd stop making so many of them," he hisses.

The anger that sweeps through me is unfamiliar and unwelcome.

"Mistakes are proof that you're living." I push back from the table. "Maybe you should try it sometime."

I stalk away, heading for the kitchen and ignore the looks I'm getting from Dad and Grayson. I'm grateful that Chrissy is still too busy with the kids for any of them to notice my exit.

Opening the refrigerator, I pull out a bottle of water and gulp it down while I try to calm down. Leaning back against the counter, I consider Tom's words, but I already know I can never live that way. Life is all about risk and reward. You don't get one without the other, and for me the ultimate reward has always been love.

We grew up watching our parents, who were as in love on the day my mom took her last breath as they were on their wedding day. Hell, my dad's love for her is still as strong nine years after her passing.

So, I know what's out there for me. I know the passion and warmth that can be found with another person and I'll risk whatever I have to, to find it.

Once I am sufficiently calm, I start to make my way

back to the dining room. I know Tom only has my best interests at heart, I just wish he'd stop being so damn judgemental.

I'm about to step out of the kitchen when my phone goes off, and when I see Charlie's name on the screen, I *know* this isn't a mistake.

Charlie: Can you meet me at 20 W Seaford Street tomorrow midday?

No, she isn't a mistake. She might possibly be the smartest chance I've ever taken.

CHAPTER SEVEN

CHARLOTTE

I glance down at my watch before looking down the street. Again. For the seventeenth time since I arrived. Three minutes ago.

Is it possible to kick your own ass? Because I'd kind of like to give it a go right now.

I'm early, I remind myself in an effort to calm my nerves. I flick my eyes anxiously up the street again just in time to see Miles round the corner, heading toward me with a grin on his face. I really like that grin, I decide. It screams devilry with a dash of roguishness, and it leaves me craving a taste of something outside my normal.

As he comes closer, I return his smile and watch his gaze sweep to the storefront behind me.

"This is what you had to show me?"

I turn and observe the shop in front of me, my mouth already salivating at the thought of what is inside, and shrug. "I've been dying to check this place out since it opened, and I figured you'd make an excellent dining companion."

"Dining companion, huh? I'm not exactly sure ice cream can be classified as a meal, Chicago, but I appreciate your passion."

My face heats at the use of the name Chicago. Nobody has ever had a pet name for me before, and while Chicago is a long way from baby or any other term of endearment, it somehow feels more personal, which makes it feel more intimate. Or I'm completely reaching, I haven't decided quite yet.

He takes hold of my hand and pulls me into the small ice creamery, which is full to the brim with people, the line almost stretching out the door. We take our spot at the end and I expect Miles to drop my hand, but he doesn't. He continues to keep our fingers entwined as though it's the most natural thing in the world. So, I ignore the insistent thrumming in my chest, follow his lead, and pretend being here with him is nothing out of the ordinary.

"How long has this place been open?" His voice is curious as he looks around and takes it all in.

"Three weeks, I think. I'm surprised you haven't heard about it, an ice cream connoisseur such as yourself," I tease.

He ducks his head looking slightly embarrassed. "Yeah, I might have a confession I need to make about that." His free hand slips into his hair, carelessly mussing it up and he looks at me nervously.

"What? You really prefer frozen yogurt? Because, I'm sorry, that's a deal breaker right there."

His eyes widen slightly, and I can't help but laugh. "I'm kidding, Miles."

"Thank fuck for that, because I hate ice cream."

The laughter dies on my lips and I stare at him with what could be something akin to horror. What kind of monster hates ice cream?

"You *hate* ice cream?"

"I do," he affirms.

"How... I mean—" I stop, unable to go on, because who is this man in front of me who hates—*hates!*—ice cream?

"You're looking at me like I just told you I hate babies." He laughs.

"Well, I mean, babies I could kind of understand. They're really too small and they cry a lot and then they can't talk so they can't tell you *why* they're crying, so I can see how that would be frustrating." I'm rambling now but I'm helpless to stop. "But what did ice cream ever do to you?"

"It's too cold." He shrugs as if that's a perfectly reasonable explanation for his insanity.

"Next, please."

We've somehow moved to the front of the line and I look at the display of ice cream and candy along the counter sadly. "We should go somewhere else," I reluctantly say.

"You're crazy if you think I'm letting you leave this shop." He gently nudges me forward. "You're staring at that ice cream the same way I look at your ass, and I refuse to be the guy who stands in the way of a love that strong."

I step forward, enjoying the flush of heat caused by his comment about my ass and order a large mint choc chip with rainbow sprinkles and gummies.

"And you, sir?" the teenage boy asks Miles in a tone that tells us he'd rather be anywhere but here right now.

"I'll take a large cup with vanilla ice cream, peanut butter cups, Kit Kats, and Swedish Fish. Minus the ice cream, please," Miles asks as though this is a perfectly normal request.

"No ice cream?" the boy asks bewildered, and Miles nods. "So, you just want a large cup of candy?"

"Yes."

He looks at Miles as though he's crazy, but he makes up both our orders without another word.

"Over there." Miles points to a small table at the back of the shop that has just become vacant and we race to claim it before someone else has a chance to grab it.

"So, you really like ice cream, huh?" He reaches across the table and snatches one of my gummies, tossing it in his mouth.

"I might have slightly overreacted." I point my plastic spoon at him. "*Slightly*. I still think it's weird that you hate ice cream and I'm questioning your trustworthiness based on this new information."

"Hmph." He grunts. "I'll win you over." He pops a peanut butter cup in his mouth and smirks at me.

"What were you doing that night at the grocery store? Stalking the dairy section for lonely women?" I raise an eyebrow at him. "If I remember correctly, and I *do*, you said you were 'passionate' about ice cream." My use of air quotes elicits an eye roll from him.

"It was a tiny white lie!" he defends. "No, seriously I might hate ice cream, but my daughter loves it, and I had promised her some for dessert."

The spoon freezes halfway to my mouth as I let that news settle over me.

Miles continues talking, oblivious to the bombshell he just dropped. "But in my defense, when you see a beautiful woman, you use whatever excuse you can to talk to her."

He has a daughter.

Suddenly his aversion to ice cream doesn't seem like such a big deal.

"You have a daughter?"

He looks across the table, meeting my eye, and nods.

"I do. Her name's Lulu. Well, it's Tallulah, but we all call her Lulu. She's two, almost three." He's watching me closely, measuring my response.

"Is she with her mom now?"

"No, my brother is watching her."

"God, please tell me you're single and I haven't just become a homewrecking hussy."

"Hussy?" He snorts. "Your good reputation is intact. I am single, I promise you. And I don't want to know what kind of men you've been dating that you even felt the need to ask that question."

"Oh, I don't date." I turn my attention back to my melting ice cream.

"You don't date?" He asks the question slowly, as

though rolling the idea on his tongue.

"Nope." I slip the spoon into my mouth and enjoy the cold slide down my throat. I may also enjoy the way Miles' eyes linger on my lips.

"Then I'm so confused about what we're doing right now."

"I mean I don't normally date," I clarify.

"Why?" It's a blunt question, but he somehow manages not to sound rude.

"I guess my job doesn't allow much time for a personal life."

"What do you do?" He bites the head of a Swedish Fish.

"Lawyer. I'm a corporate lawyer."

"Ah, well, that makes sense. I can see how it could make things hard."

I swirl my ice cream around the cup and look at him thoughtfully. "I would say the same thing about being a dad. Although I guess you have some time for dating when she's with her mom?" *God, subtle, Charlie. Real subtle.*

"Her mom passed away."

Jesus, I guess Miles has declared today drop-a-bomb-Saturday or something.

"I'm so sorry, I shouldn't have even mentioned her, it's really none of my bus—" I'm flustered so I cut myself off to try and regroup. "I'm sorry for your loss."

"It's fine, Charlie, really." He reaches across the table and slips his fingers in between mine. "We weren't a couple. Renee was one of my best friends, had been since college, but there was never anything romantic between us. One night, we had a bit too much to drink and two months later we were staring at a stick covered in her pee, realizing that our lives were about to change forever." He shakes his head with a grin. Is he ever *not* smiling? "At the time, it felt a hell of a lot less clichéd than it sounds."

"I can't even imagine." And I couldn't. Kids were unapologetically not in my life plan.

"I feel like things have taken a turn into the too-serious-for-a-first-date zone, Chicago. Especially one in a shop with an ice cream wearing a top hat painted on the window." He nods toward the illustration painted on the large shop front window. "How about if, just for the afternoon, we pretend that our lives are completely uncomplicated, and we spend the next few hours enjoying each other?"

"And when the afternoon is over?" I can't stop the question from forming on my lips.

"We decide if what this is, is worth facing reality for." He shrugs and looks at me with an expression so full of hope that all I want to do is agree. Because, despite the complexity of our situations, I am so not ready to walk away from this.

"Okay, explain the rationale behind the ice cream thing, and I want a proper answer this time, my decision might depend on it."

Two hours later, I'm laughing helplessly as Miles defends his—some might say unhealthy—obsession with Sandra Bullock.

"Okay, you need to calm down." He glares at me

across the table. "It's not an *obsession*, and it's the movies I love. Not *her*."

"You just told me you had her posters all over your wall!" I argue, trying desperately to keep a straight face.

"When I was a *teenager*. And you swore you would never repeat that." A scowl settles on his face.

I push away the chocolate shake in front of me and hold my arms up. "Sorry, I'm sorry! But in my defense, you really shouldn't tell anyone that." I level him with a fierce glare. "Ever."

"Hmph, I'm secure enough in my masculinity to own it. Come at me, Chicago, I can take anything you throw at me." He winks at me and takes a huge gulp of his own milkshake. *Strawberry*. I'm seriously questioning our compatibility right now.

Taking a look around the still busy shop, I glance at a pair of women sitting by the front window. Both beautiful, they are the type of women who intimidate the hell out of me. Long-limbed, perfectly made-up faces, and that air of confidence that comes with knowing wherever you go, you are wanted and welcomed.

They have also been throwing subtle glances our way since they sat down and it's starting to set my nerves on edge.

"What about you?" Miles' deep voice interrupts my thoughts. "You must have some embarrassing stories. It's only fair," he goads.

"Oh God, not really." I consider his question. Of course, I have plenty of mortifying teenage stories I could tell him. Doesn't mean I'm going to. I might not do this whole dating thing often, but I'm not stupid.

"Okay, I will admit to being a bit pop-music obsessed," I admit. "In high school, my best friend and I used to spend hours trying to recreate the Backstreet Boys' dance routines. I still say they are musical geniuses and never got the credit they deserve." He opens his mouth to interrupt, but I quickly cut him off. "Disagreeing with me really doesn't bode well for you here, so think carefully before you speak."

Miles leans back in his seat and folds his arms across his chest. His extremely broad chest. *Le sigh.*

"I couldn't agree with you more."

"Good answer, sir. Good answer." I raise my glass to him.

"So, that's it?" He shakes his head sadly. "My stories were much more embarrassing than that. I'm kind of disappointed in you."

I throw a wadded-up napkin at him, but he ducks and I miss, the napkin instead landing by the feet of the girls at the table who have been ogling Miles.

My eyes narrow when I see them still watching, having now lost all pretense of subterfuge.

"What just happened here?"

"Huh?" I drag my attention from blonde one and blonde two, back to him.

"Your face just went all…" He scrunches his nose up, as though he smelled something revolting.

"No, it didn't," I counter with the confidence of a lawyer who is used to faking it when needed.

"Saying it didn't doesn't make it true, you know. But since it's only our first date, I'll let it slide. Now tell me what caused that expression of pure delight."

"Ugh," I sigh. "Okay, there's something you should know about me."

"Okay." Miles leans forward, a look of wariness sliding across his features.

"I don't really people very well." My shoulders sag, such is my relief at getting this off my chest.

"You don't *people* well?" His brow creases. "I'm not sure I know what that means."

"I'm not good with people. I find most of them irritating and confusing a lot of the time. It's exhausting, really."

"Don't lawyers have to *people* a lot?" he asks curiously.

"Yep." I pop the sound of the P. "So much peopling. Which makes my threshold for it even lower on my off time."

"Is this your polite way of saying you're sick of me and it's time to call it a day?"

"No," I laugh. "Not at all. I've just been putting up with those two girls eyeing you like you're their first coffee of the day for the last two hours."

He turns and glances behind him just in time to see blonde one wink at him.

Are you kidding me right now?

When he shifts in his seat to look at me, his whole demeanor has changed and a sudden flutter of nerves hits me.

Miles reaches up and begins to play with his empty glass before casting an anxious look my way.

"There's something you need to know."

CHAPTER EIGHT

"Hello, Detective." Adelaide opens the door to her apartment with Lucifer's trademark greeting, including her—very bad—attempt at an English accent. "I thought you were going to come at five?"

I push past her, my arms full with a container of my homemade choc chunk marshmallow cookies and a bottle of coffee liqueur for the many, *many* White Russians I plan on drinking tonight. "I'm only a little late."

Addy grabs the liqueur bottle and heads to her tiny kitchenette, pointing to her laden coffee table.

"Put the cookies with the rest of the food. The next episode is queued up, just give me a sec to get you a drink."

I flop onto her sofa with a loud grunt and slide my Tupperware container in between a bowl of peanut M&M's and what looks to be Adelaide's favorite chocolate peanut butter cupcakes. I use my finger to scoop up a bit of icing and savor the creamy peanut butter deliciousness.

"Hey, where's the ice cream?" I shout, only to jump when Adelaide appears by my elbow, handing me my drink.

"I forgot to pick it up, you'll have to make do without tonight. Deal with it."

Today is really not a good day for ice cream.

"So." She curls up next to me and points the remote at the television, bringing it to life. "How did today go?"

"It was…" I search for the right words and find myself coming up short.

"That does not sound promising." Her wide blue eyes fill with sympathy. I hate it.

"It wasn't bad." I try to sound more confident than I feel as I stuff a cookie in my mouth.

"But it wasn't good?"

"No, it was. It was just— He has a kid."

Addy stops mid-chew. "Oh, shit. You, my love, are not a kid person, you know that, right?"

"Yes, Adelaide, thank you, I am well aware."

"What are you going to do?"

"I don't know." I take a big gulp of my drink and contemplate how nice it is that there is such a thing as what is essentially an alcoholic coffee. "I really like him. He's funny and he makes me feel comfortable. It's like he cuts my awkward in half."

"Plus, he's hot, right?"

"God, *so* hot," I agree.

A loud bang out in the hallway, followed by laughter, interrupts us and Addy rolls her eyes and mutters under her breath.

"Oh my God, is that him?" I bolt upright. "Is that your friendly neighborhood douchebag?" She pulls the bowl of M&M's onto her lap and begins shoveling them into her mouth.

"I'll take that as a yes." I laugh and jump up, racing to the door to peer out the peephole. I'm too late though, and the hallway is empty.

"Get your ass back here and sit down, will ya. We were in the middle of a conversation."

"You have complained about this guy every day since he moved in four months ago—"

"Six months. It's been six months."

I snatch some candy out of the bowl on her lap. "Six months then. When are you going to ask him out?"

"Uh, never. The guy's an obnoxious ass who thinks he's God's gift to women." She sits up straighter, her eyes lighting up. "Did I tell you he had the nerve to accuse me of stealing his mail as an excuse to talk to him?" Her voice is getting louder and taking on a screechy quality. "I mean, I try to do the right thing when his stupid mail was put in my box and that's how he thanks me! Such an asshole." She points a hand full of candy at me. "And don't change the subject, Charlie. We were talking about Miles. Are you gonna call him Daddy?" She waggles her eyebrows at me.

"That is wrong on so many levels, how broken are you?"

"Ugh, relax. I know you're not a daddy-kink type of

girl. Although you shouldn't knock it until you've tried it."

"Why am I friends with you?"

"Because I'm the only one who will put up with you." I keep quiet because she's probably right. "Now, what is the plan for Miles. Please don't tell me you're going to dick out because of the kid? I don't want to have to smack you."

"No, I mean, maybe, I don't kno— Wait, dick out?"

She sighs deeply. "Everyone says don't pussy out but really, pussies are tough as shit. Dicks are fragile, so saying don't dick out makes way more sense." She shrugs as if that makes complete sense and for a moment I wonder if we've been friends for too long, because it kind of does.

I shake my head and try to refocus. "I don't want kids. I never wanted kids. My job is too demanding, too time-consuming. Kids make no sense for me and it's stupid to even consider going any further with this because it can't possibly go anywhere now."

"But?" Addy's foot nudges me gently.

"It sounds ridiculous, I don't want to say it out loud." My hand finds my drink and I take a grateful sip.

"But you will, so you might as well just spit it out."

"I feel at home with him." Those words make me feel remarkably helpless. "I had my life figured out. I knew what I needed out of life to make me feel safe." I bite my lip and the sting distracts me for a moment. "It's not this."

"Forget safe, Charlie. *Fuck safe*. Life isn't about being safe. It's about getting messy and taking chances and *experiencing* everything." She scoots closer toward me and grips my calf. "I've watched you for the past three years. You work, you go home where you work some more, binge-watch sitcoms and sexy demons— Oh!" She turns and pauses the television which had been forgotten. "You sleep, and then you get up and do it all over again. I manage to get your ass here once a month for a girls' night and that's it. That's the extent of your social life. Honestly, it's a miracle you even met Miles!" She throws her hands up dramatically.

"That's not true. I went to New York to visit Wyatt not long ago. And I'm going to that gala in a couple of weeks. I have a social life." I try not to sound defensive. I fail.

"You went to New York eight months ago and the gala is a work function. That does not equate to a social life, my love. I'm sorry, just, no."

"What would you do?"

"Me?" She sighs deeply. "I'd jump into it headfirst, kid and all. But you're not me and that's okay, Charlie. Being you is okay."

Why do you always ruin everything? The memory twists deep within me.

"Right." I snort. "You would be the only one to think so." I turn to face her. "What should I do?"

"I think you should take it slow. Just get to know him and don't worry about the other stuff. At least, not until you're sure this is going somewhere. *Then* you can figure the rest out." She tilts her head to the side. "What's the worst that can happen?"

"I could get my heart broken," I offer.

"Meh, no one ever died from a broken heart." She throws an M&M at me, so I retaliate with the plump cushion from behind my back. My aim is off though and it sails over her shoulder.

"That wasn't his only revelation, by the way."

A television begins blaring from the apartment belonging to Adelaide's nightmare neighbor.

"Does he always have his TV so loud?" I question, straining to make out the overexcited babbling coming from the too-loud television.

"He's an inconsiderate jerk, so yes." She returns the bowl of candy to the coffee table, swapping it for a cupcake. "What else did he say?"

"Well, he hates ice cream." The cupcake stops midair, its path to Addy's mouth halted while she looks at me incredulously.

"He *hates* ice cream?"

"Yes! That's weird, right?" My words are tinged with vindication. I *knew* it was strange.

"I mean, yeah, it's unusual, but if you think I'm going to tell you to stop seeing him over *ice cream*, you're out of your freaking mind." She takes a bite of the cake and mumbles around her mouthful. "Stop trying to find excuses to give up on this."

"Fine." I huff. "Anyway, that wasn't the weirdest thing he told me. He was on a reality show last year." I groan.

"Wait, what?" Adelaide blurts and then she starts coughing as she chokes on her cupcake.

I reach over and give her a couple of hard thumps on her back and give her a moment to recover.

"I thought you'd like that." Adelaide is obsessed with reality television. Housewives, dancers, survivors, drag queens, she watches them all.

"Which show was he on?" she asks excitedly.

"Marrying the MILF? No, wait, MILF is a mother, right?" God, what was it called?

"*Dating the DILF?*"

"Yeah, that's it. Did you watch it?" I grab a cupcake and use my finger to scoop half the icing off, licking it clean.

"You're dating Miles *Kent* from *Dating the DILF?*"

"I had *a* date with him. Why are you looking at me like that?" Her eyes are narrowed, and she looks almost worried.

"What did he tell you about the show?"

"Not much. Just that it wasn't a very good experience and he regrets doing it. Why?"

"Yeah, I bet he does." Her lips are pursed, and she looks pissed. "Okay, I might need to reevaluate my opinion, Charlie. I know he seems like a catch, but I think maybe you're right. The kid thing is probably a deal breaker, so there's really no point in pursuing it." She nods her head firmly as though the discussion is over and grabs the remote.

"What aren't you telling me?" I could not possibly be more confused by her change of heart.

"Look, I don't want to say too much, because I know those shows are exaggerated and it's really all about ratings, but I think you should google hi—" She's cut off by a rhythmic banging that starts up on the wall behind the television. The same wall that Adelaide shares with her neighbor from hell.

"You have *got* to be kidding me," she exclaims and bolts up, storming toward the door.

Throwing my cake down on the table, I jump up and follow her, trying to talk her out of doing anything stupid, but also a little bit thrilled to get a peek at the guy who has been driving her so crazy.

She bangs on his door with two hands and I take a step back because I have never seen Addy so riled up before. She's kind of frightening.

The door opens and a tall guy with messy blond hair and a smile that screams danger stands there, his stormy gray eyes taking in every inch of her, from her jean-short-clad legs to the messy bun on top of her head.

He clearly likes what he sees.

"What can I do for you tonight, princess?"

"Don't call me that," she snaps. "And you can try keeping it down in there. Like maybe turn the television down and not throw things against the wall? That'd be great, m'kay?" She starts to spin around, but he grabs her wrist and stops her.

"I'm sorry, Adelaide." His face the picture of contrition. "My niece is here, and I have trouble saying no to her. But for you, I will incur her wrath. I really am sorry."

I cross my arms over my chest and bite my lip to stop my laughter, enjoying the show.

"Fine." Addy's shoulders slump slightly as though

the fight has left her body. "Thank you." She turns back to me. "C'mon, let's go."

I'm about to follow when I glance into the apartment behind neighbor-guy and see a familiar face walk into the kitchen.

"Miles?"

CHAPTER NINE

I look up at the sound of my name and come face to face with a confused Charlie. I'm pretty sure my expression mirrors hers.

What is she doing at Grayson's place?

A smaller, pixie-faced blonde suddenly appears in front of Charlie and her eyes narrow shrewdly as she appraises me. Yeah, it's safe to say, she recognizes me.

Gray is watching us all, his brows drawn together and wearing a small frown.

"That's Charlie," I inform him.

"Really?" He turns to her with a broad grin. "How's your pussy?"

"Excuse me?" Her lips flatten into a straight line.

"Your cat." He shifts back in my direction. "Didn't you say she found a cat?"

The blonde murmurs something under her breath and I'm pretty sure I catch the word asshole.

"That's Adelaide," Gray tells me. Ah, the neighbor

he's been after since he moved in. The animosity makes sense now. Maybe she doesn't recognize me after all.

"Well, well, well, if it isn't the DILF who's dating my friend."

Fuck me.

"Aren't you going to invite us in?" Adelaide addresses Grayson.

"I've been inviting you in for six months, princess. You finally going to take me up on my offer?"

"Nope, but I will come in." She grabs a bewildered-looking Charlie and drags her inside.

The last few minutes have been complete confusion, but a silence settles over all of us when a small but mighty voice calls out from the living room.

"Daddy, where's the pizza?"

We all turn and look at Lulu, whose eyes have not lifted from her coloring, despite the noise we've been making.

"It'll be here soon, kid, I promise."

"And cheesy bread?" she prompts with a childish lilt.

"Yeah, and cheesy bread."

"'Kay."

"I think we should go." Charlie watches Lulu, who continues to ignore us, with a panicked look on her face before turning to Adelaide. "Addy, we need to go."

Adelaide bites her lip and nods. "Okay."

"Don't go." They both look at me with surprise. I'm pretty fucking shocked myself. I don't introduce women to Lulu, it's my number one dating rule, but Chicago has me wanting to break all the rules.

"You should definitely stay," Gray backs me up, although my guess is, he has his own ulterior motives. "We have pizza coming and it's just four friends hanging out as far as Nugget is concerned. It's not a big deal." He shrugs.

"Excuse us one moment." Charlie pulls Adelaide back out into the hallway and they launch into a whispered conversation full of animated expressions and energetic hand flailing. Finally, Charlie nods her head and makes her way back to me.

She stops in front of me while I lean against the doorframe and looks up at me apprehensively.

"I'm not much of a kid person, so please don't hold it against me if she hates me." She chews on her bottom lip. "I thought I'd have more time to prepare for this."

I glance over my shoulder to make sure Lulu is still distracted and take a step forward, so we're shielded by the door.

"Lulu loves everyone, trust me, you don't have anything to worry about." I take her hand and pull her to me, leaning down until my mouth is a breath away from hers. "I had a really great time today and this is a pretty damn amazing coincidence. We would be stupid not to take advantage of it." My mouth presses softly against hers and I sweep my tongue along her bottom lip. When her lips part and her tongue slides along mine, my cock jerks against my jeans, an uncomfortable reminder that I need to be careful tonight in front of Lulu. The smallest touch from Charlie seems to overwhelm me. It's too much and not enough all at once.

A gruff clearing of a throat breaks the moment and I look up to see the pizza guy standing there, shifting uncomfortably.

"Uh, delivery for Grayson?"

Gray pushes past us, making sure to brush against Adelaide on the way. She glares at his back and I decide that I'm a little afraid of her.

"Ignore those two. I keep telling him, she's your sister, man, you can't kiss her like that in public." He rolls his eyes in mock annoyance and slips some cash to the slack-jawed delivery guy, before ushering us all inside the apartment.

"You're a freak," I mutter, flitting my eyes across to Charlie to make sure he hasn't scared her off. Luckily for Gray, she is wearing a small smile and tucking a lock of hair behind her ear. Maybe his bad joke was enough to break the tension?

We all follow Gray into the small living room where he drops the pizzas on the coffee table alongside a pile of paper plates.

"Dig in," he instructs. "I'll get some sodas."

"Water for Lulu," I remind him.

"For duck's sake!"

We all turn and stare wide-eyed at my daughter. My perfect, angelic baby girl who apparently has cracked the curse word code at the tender age of two and three quarters.

"Tallulah!" I scold at the same time Gray offers her a high-five and says, "Nice!"

"What?" I seethe.

"What?" he repeats innocently. "Last week I heard her say…" He lowers his voice to a whisper. "The F-word. So, I taught her a more socially acceptable version. You should be thanking me."

A snort comes from across the table and I look up to find Charlie and Adelaide desperately trying to disguise their laughter.

I shake my head and try my best to hide my own amusement. I swear to God, half of parenting is covering up how funny you find their behavior.

Turning to Lulu, I get her attention. "Kid, don't ever listen to anything your uncle Gray tells you, understand?"

She considers me thoughtfully and I can see the cogs of her brain turning. "Unstand. Can I have soda?"

"No."

Lulu throws herself dramatically on the floor, groaning.

"Lu, sit up so you can meet our friends." The mention of friends has her sitting straight up and taking notice of Charlie and Adelaide for the first time. I introduce them both to her and she gets up and wanders around the table to stand in front of them.

I can't help but hold my breath. I know what I said but if she doesn't like Charlie that would make things considerably harder on us. And from the reaction I got from Adelaide before, I would say we already have that against us.

Lulu ignores Adelaide and locks eyes with Charlie, who is staring at her wide-eyed and as still as a statue.

She looks too scared to breathe and I cover my mouth to hide a grin.

"You're pretty."

"Thank you."

"I am too." Lulu tilts her head to the side and flattens her mouth.

Charlie's alarmed eyes fly to mine. "Yes, you are."

"I know." She shrugs. "I like your bracelet." Her fingers reach out to touch the delicate silver thread on Charlie's wrist. "Can I wear it?"

"I'd rather you didn't." Lulu's mouth drops slightly, along with my stomach.

"Why?"

Charlie crosses her legs and shifts until she's comfortable. "Because it was a gift from my nanna and poppa and it's very special to me."

Lulu's eyes light up. "My gramps gives me presents too. Look!" She sticks out her wrist where a gaudy bright pink plastic watch rests.

"Oh, uh, it's very nice."

"Yup. It's my favorite." And just like that, Lulu plops herself in Charlie's lap and begins chatting away. I have to fight back a laugh at the startled look on Charlie's face.

"Here you go." Gray sets down some cans of soda on the table and takes a seat next to Adelaide.

"Were you guys settling in for a marathon of… what is this?" Adelaide asks, staring at the blaring television.

"It's *The JoJo and BowBow Show*," I manage to get out. The show is fucking ridiculous, but Lulu is obsessed with it at the moment. "And, no. We had a deal, she got the TV until the pizza arrived and then it was ours for the night."

Lulu stops her chatter and glares at me, before going right back to extolling the virtues of the Barbie Dreamhouse she has asked for, for her birthday.

"It was Miles' turn to pick the movie tonight, so you're in for a treat," Gray teases.

"Actually, I've changed my mind." I run a hand through my hair nervously and glance over at Charlie to see her watching me with eyes alight with humor.

"Oh, no, don't change your mind on our account." She laughs. "I have a feeling I'll get so much enjoyment from your choice. Play it, Grayson."

"As you wish." It's my turn to glare now as he pulls up the movie and Charlie bursts into giggles when the opening credits for *While You Were Sleeping* start rolling.

"It's a good movie," I grumble.

An hour later, Lulu is fast asleep on the sofa and we are in the middle of debating the merits of Jack and Peter and who Lucy should have chosen.

"I'm never going to agree with you all. Peter was an upstanding dude and Lucy was making him a better man. She should have gone through with the wedding," Gray insists. "And don't even get me started on that meddling Saul. He should have kept his nose right out of it."

Adelaide throws popcorn at him with a groan.

"What about you, Charlie? Please tell me you're on the side of right and agree that Jack was the only choice?"

She takes a gulp of soda before answering. "He's the rational choice, and I judge anyone who disagrees." She quirks an eyebrow at Gray.

She has impressed me tonight. After some initial awkwardness she relaxed enough to enjoy a laugh with Gray, and I loved watching her with Lulu. She didn't talk down to her or baby her at all, which is a mistake a lot of people make. Lulu is around adults the majority of time, so she's used to being treated like a miniature grown-up. She doesn't respond well when she's suddenly treated like the kid she is. Right or wrong, it's the way it is and it's as though Charlie instinctively understood that.

"Okay, now that the kid is asleep and we've had a bit of a laugh, I think it's time to get a bit serious."

We all turn to Adelaide as she spouts off her ominous warning and she looks me dead in the eye.

"You were quite the prick on that show."

"It definitely appeared that way."

"Appeared? You're saying it wasn't a true depiction of you?"

"It wasn't."

"Hmm, well, I mean, that's easy to say. Are we just supposed to trust you?"

"Honestly, I don't really care if you trust me." I shrug apologetically. "I care if Charlie trusts me, and I'm under no illusion that's going to happen just because I tell her she can. But I *will* prove it to her."

Charlie's wide eyes are bouncing between the two of us while Gray watches with an amused smile.

Adelaide pops a piece of popcorn in her mouth and

chews slowly, staring at me contemplatively. "Fine, you have my approval." She nods decisively and turns to Charlie. "I know I said you should google him, but don't, okay?"

"Oh God, yeah, for the love of Christ, do not google him."

"Do not google me, it will only end in tears. Mine."

Gray and I quickly jump in, talking over each other the moment Adelaide mentions google.

Charlie looks uncertain and I hate that she feels that way about me. For the millionth time, I wish I could turn back time and erase that stupid show from my history.

"Okay, I won't," she agrees and although she doesn't look completely convinced, I'm grateful she is prepared to take a chance on me.

I check my watch and see that it's only seven-thirty, so I suggest another movie. "I'll even let you choose." I nod toward the girls.

"Just one more thing," Adelaide says, looking at Charlie pointedly. "Charlie has a cocktail party on the fourteenth and she needs a date. Are you available?"

"I most definitely am."

"Excellent. Pick her up at seven. She'll text you her address."

"Are you two done planning out my personal life?" Charlie asks in exasperation and Adelaide and I grin at each other.

"Yep," we both agree.

"Right, I'm so glad you guys have sorted that out, now, Charlie, I have an important question and I need an answer because it's been bothering me ever since Miles told me about it." We all look at Gray, the girls with curiosity and me with dread. He smirks back at us.

"Really, how is your pussy?"

CHAPTER TEN

CHARLOTTE

I zip up my makeup bag and give myself a final once-over in the bathroom mirror, once again cursing the terrible bathroom lighting. I really should do something about that.

My heart is hammering nervously, and I check my phone for the time. Ten minutes until Miles arrives.

The last few weeks have been wonderful. While we haven't had a lot of opportunities to see each other, we have spoken or messaged daily and I have a feeling we are beyond the point of no return. Meeting Lulu so early was a shock, and if I think about that night, I can still feel the terror that overwhelmed me when I first laid eyes on her. I'm not sure how normal it is to be so scared of a toddler, but that two-foot-tall, blonde-haired, blue-eyed angel was pretty much my worst nightmare.

Miles has also since admitted that he was nervous, which doesn't surprise me. There's no denying that if

Lulu hated me, which I had fully expected, whatever this is between us would have been over.

Thankfully, that wasn't the case and I'm pretty sure I sealed the deal when I heard her whisper a quiet *sit*, which I have no doubt was meant to be *shit*, when she spilled her water on the sofa. Keeping my mouth shut probably wasn't my finest adulting moment, but a prospective girlfriend has to do what a prospective girlfriend has to do.

Once I have tidied up the bathroom, I pull my phone out, fully intending to check the time again, but instead I pull up my texts and find my thread with Miles.

Reading back over our messages evokes a swirl of emotions within me. There are the usual nerves I feel when getting to know someone new, alongside the fear I associate with opening myself up to someone. The anxiety that worms its way into my brain, reminding me that one day, whether it be a week from now, or a year, he will walk away. Because I am a ruiner and I destroy everything I love.

But lately, there has been something else. Something that has been driving me through the apprehension and coaxing me through my misgivings.

Hope for a future I never thought I was built for.

I let my eyes linger on the messages I received earlier this afternoon and my pulse picks up, thrumming loudly in my ears.

· · ·

Miles: Dad is taking Lulu for the night, so I have no curfew.

Miles: Did you hear that? It was my freedom war cry lol

I never replied. I wasn't able to think of anything that would be sufficiently flirty, so I went with silence. You can't go wrong with silence, right?

Oh, God, how is it possible to be *this* bad at dating?

The sound of the doorbell snaps me out of my internal hatefest and I race down the stairs as fast as my heels allow. Taking a moment before I open the door, I take a deep breath and release it slowly, hoping it will settle my nerves.

When I open the door, a heavy silence sits between us. What was I thinking earlier about silence being bad? Because there's nothing bad about this. It's loaded with heat and bursting with a ferocity I have never experienced before.

"Wow." He breaks the silence and a flush colors my face.

He's standing on my front porch with a look of appreciation on his face and I wonder if he can see that same appreciation reflected back. Because Miles in a suit is a sight to behold.

From the navy-blue blazer that fits his broad chest and shoulders impeccably, to the shiny black oxfords on his feet, he is picture-perfect deliciousness.

He leans down and places a kiss just below my ear and the spicy notes of his aftershave hit me at the same time as his lips. It's enough to make a girl weak at the knees.

"You look incredible." His hand is still holding on to my arm, his fingers curled around my elbow. Are elbows an erogenous zone, because it's feeling pretty damn sensual right about now.

Trying to stop that train of thought, I smooth my hands over my red sheath dress. "Give me one second, I just need to grab my clutch."

He steps into the entrance and my little gray furball appears from nowhere and begins winding its way between his legs. Miles bends down to pick him up.

"That ear healed up well." He nuzzles the cat.

"It did, and he was so good while it was healing."

"She." Miles chuckles.

"Oh, right, *she*." I roll my eyes. "So, I finally decided on a name," I call out, heading into the kitchen to grab my bag.

"Jesus, it's about time. What did you go with?"

I quickly open my clutch and slide my phone inside, making sure I have some cash, my debit card, and my ID.

"Mintie." I walk back into the entrance to see Miles looking at the photo of my grandparents I keep there. "It seemed appropriate when I busted him eating from my bowl of ice cream last night."

I step toward him and lean down to place a kiss on Mintie's head, and when I look up, I am only inches away from Miles. He takes advantage by brushing a kiss against my mouth.

His hand lands on my waist and slides down to

settle on my ass, grabbing a handful of my butt cheek. A jolt of heat rushes through me and I step even closer, pressing my body to his, and thread my hands through his hair. He deepens the kiss, and in a moment of clit-aching perfection, sucks lightly on my tongue before pulling back to nibble along my bottom lip.

I can feel him harden against my stomach and for the first time in my life I'm ready to throw out the rules and blow off my responsibilities. I am about to suggest just that when there is an angry hiss between us, and we jump apart.

Mintie leaps from Miles' arms and stalks off, throwing a look of disdain back at us.

Miles clears his throat and looks at me in amusement. "I guess we should get going?"

The distance has done its job and cleared my head, so I nod, not trusting my voice right now, and as I lock up and follow Miles to his car, I let my mind wander to how the night might end. Or more specifically, how I hope it will end.

"I thought you didn't like peopling?" Miles' deep voice questions.

We're walking through the vast ballroom of a downtown hotel, where my firm is holding its annual client gala. The night has managed to be both draining, as these nights usually are, and absurdly wonderful all at once.

"I said I didn't like it, not that I wasn't great at it." I lean into his solid form and take a sip of champagne.

His arm winds around me, his hand settling on my waist and he gives a gentle squeeze. "You'd never know. You're working the room like you own it."

"It will take me a week to recover from all this," I assure him. "Poor Addy will have to run interference so I have to talk to as few people as possible."

"I'm surprised she's not here."

I'm momentarily distracted by Tiff Klein, the wife of one of our biggest clients, whose gaze is fixed on Miles, her nose slightly wrinkled in a look of distaste.

It has been an ongoing theme tonight. The women in the room have definitely been taking note of his appearance and while, in general, it has been a pervasive sense of subtle curiosity, I have recognized a few ladies looking with either fierce interest or deep hostility. It has me slightly on edge.

"These events aren't mandatory for assistants." I force myself to ignore Mrs. Klein. "It's strongly encouraged that they attend, but it's Addy's mom's birthday today, so she's having dinner with her family."

His grip on me tightens and he leans down, his lips finding my ear. "I'm glad I could be here with you tonight, then."

How does he know? How does this guy that I have only known for a month seem to understand me as well as he does? Because I can do this thing tonight. I can absolutely come in with my game face on and I can impress every single person who needs to be impressed. But every second is filled with anxiety, and if I had had to do this alone tonight, it would have seemed insurmountable.

"I'm glad too."

"Charlotte." My boss appears suddenly in front of us, startling me, and I take a step away from Miles as I remember I really should entertain some decorum considering where we are. Despite the free-flowing alcohol and all the schmoozing, this is essentially a night at the office.

"Kendall," I greet her. "Miles, you remember my boss, Kendall Harris." He nods at her with a polite smile, which she does her best to return, but her face is taut and filled with tension.

"Charlotte, David Brennan is insisting that the draft of the contract be emailed over to his partner now."

I know the contract she's referring to. A team of us spent today locked up in a hotel room with Mr. Brennan negotiating the finer points of the agreement.

"I thought we were going to finalize it tomorrow and send it through?"

"So did I." Kendall's lips purse. "Apparently he wants his business partner to review it before we go any further." She shakes her head in annoyance. "Would you mind running up to the room and emailing it through?" She hands me the room key. "Send it to their corporate office in LA. The number is on the contract."

"Of course." She's moved on before I can say anything else, so I turn to Miles and offer him an apologetic smile. "I'm sorry."

"Don't worry about it." He takes my hand, entwining our fingers. "Lead the way."

"Are you sure? I don't mind if you would rather wait at the bar? I won't be long."

"I'd rather be with you."

I search his eyes for any sign of annoyance at this disruption, but I find none.

"Okay, let's get this over with and then the next round of drinks are on me."

"It's an open bar, Chicago," he counters wryly.

"Jeez, appreciate the gesture, will you." I roll my eyes at him and start for the elevators, but I come to a sharp stop when Miles fails to move.

I turn, confused, and Miles' eyes, which only moments before were playful, are now watching me earnestly. He takes a step closer and drops my hand, lifting both of his to cradle my face.

"I appreciate everything about you." And he presses a kiss to my lips that has my thighs clenching together in an effort to control my altogether inappropriate response to his mouth on mine.

Pulling away, he maintains his hold of me and slays me with a wicked smirk.

"C'mon, let's see what trouble we can find in this hotel room."

He stalks off, pulling me behind him as a throb pulses through my core at the promise his words hold, all thoughts of decorum and etiquette vanishing.

CHAPTER ELEVEN

CHARLOTTE

The hotel is humming around us, the air thick with the heady anticipation of a Saturday night as people make their way through the palatial lobby.

Miles hasn't said a word since he pulled me from the ballroom, and my mind is working overtime, playing his words over and over.

"What floor?" His resonant voice pulls me out of my head.

"Hmm?"

"Which floor are we going to?" Bemusement colors his words.

"Oh, fifteen." I clear my throat and ignore his smirk.

Nothing is going to happen, I tell myself. That would be the height of inappropriateness and… and it would just be so *wrong*!

"You're looking a little flushed there, Charlie. You okay?" Miles is watching me with a look that tells me he knows damn well what is going through my mind right now.

"Fine." I keep my answer short and sweet since I seem to be experiencing some difficulty controlling my breathing.

"If you say so." The smirk is still there, a dirty salute to promises begging to be kept.

I'm just not sure who will be doing the begging.

He turns his attention to the display above the doors, watching the numbers rise.

I should make something clear. I am, by no means, a prude. I *love* sex and I'm a firm believer that an orgasm a day keeps the stress at bay. But—but, not butt, *that* is a no-go zone, sorry, boys—I'm the first to admit, I'm not the most adventurous in that area and I have never been with anyone who *wanted* to experiment.

In college it was clumsy fumblings, get it in and out before a roommate walked in on us. And, after? Well, there hasn't actually been many after. Relationships never worked out well for me. There was too much drama, too much turmoil. When I discovered my first post-college boyfriend was cheating on me, I was devastated. When I discovered that he was cheating on me with his girlfriend and *I* was actually the other woman, I was livid. I found myself wallowing in bed, wavering between heartbreak and hatred with a pint of ice cream and a bottle of five-dollar wine. Sucking down that wine in a bed strewn with dirty tissues and melted ice cream all over the sheets was the moment I realized history was repeating itself. How many times had my mother locked herself away, crying over some idiot who had broken her heart, only to dust herself off and find herself in exactly the same situation months later.

I decided right then that wasn't going to be me. Those emotional extremes that only served to remind me of my turbulent childhood weren't what I wanted. Stability and balance was what I needed to find my peace, and that is what I crave more than anything.

So, why am I standing here next to a man who is everything I shouldn't want and, instead of running away, I'm desperate for him in every way.

I want to break every one of my rules for him and with him. I want that strange, little, cussing human of his to like me, because she came from him and every part of him is important to me. Even the parts that terrify me.

The elevator doors ding open and we both step out of the small space. I turn to head toward room 1514, but Miles stops me, taking hold of my wrist lightly.

"I would never expect you to do anything you don't want to. You know that, right?"

His thumb is rubbing slow circles over the tender flesh of my wrist and he's looking at me so sincerely. I know he's being honest, and I don't have a moment of doubt that, while he may push my boundaries in many different ways, he will never exploit my trust.

"I know."

"Good, because it was just a stupid joke. Our first time together isn't going to be during a few stolen moments at your work party." He places a kiss on my forehead, then moves his mouth to my ear, lowering his voice to a husky whisper. "We'll need all night for everything I have planned. Now…" Taking a step back, he nods in the direction I was heading. "This way?"

Ignoring the flush of disappointment that courses through me—what is *wrong* with me?—I murmur a quick affirmation and a few minutes later we are entering the hotel room.

"I'll just be a minute. Grab something from the minibar if you want, no one will ever know." I race to the large mahogany desk on the other side of the room, and using an app on my phone, I quickly scan the document I need and email it.

Duty done, I turn back to Miles, eager to get back to the party and enjoy the rest of the night.

He's standing in front of the full-length window that spans an entire wall of the room, his eyes glued to the view. The city below us is lit up and glowing. It's truly a sight to behold.

"It's so beautiful." I move to stand next to him.

"It is," he agrees, but when I look up at him, his eyes are no longer on the vista below us.

I want to kiss him. I want to do a lot more than kiss him, but it seems like a good place to start. So, just like with everything else involving this man, I give in to the urge and take hold of his lapels, pulling him down until we are eye to eye.

"Don't let me regret this." It's a plea, for more than just this moment, but a pointless one. I couldn't stop any of it from happening, even if I wanted to.

And, let me make it very clear. I don't.

His eyes dance over my face, as if reassuring himself of my intention and then his mouth is on mine, his tongue licking along my bottom lip, seeking entry. I open for him, ready to taste him. I'm desperate to feel his tongue, his mouth, on every inch of my flesh and I wrap my arms around his neck, pulling him closer, as close as I can get.

He turns us around, pushing my back up against the window and pressing the length of his body into me, until I feel the obscene thrust of his cock against my stomach. The need to grind my body against his is urgent and consuming, and when I hear the low growl he emits, I do it all over again.

His hand threads through my hair and he pulls back sharply, exposing the curve of my neck to his greedy mouth. He bites and sucks, using his tongue to soothe the sting.

"Are you sure?" His lips move against the skin of my throat and it tickles. I try to find a way to tell him I have never been more sure of anything in my life, without actually saying the words, because he has rendered me speechless right now.

Instead, I simply nod and begin undoing the buttons on his shirt, but he stops me and takes a slight step back.

We hold each other's gaze, while my heart thuds against my chest. I know what he's doing. Giving me a moment to gather myself, free of his touch, to be sure of the decision I'm making.

Don't let me regret this.

I twist my arm behind my back and slowly lower

the zipper, being sure to hold his eye the entire time, and then let my dress fall to the ground.

He grits out a guttural groan at the sight of me, completely naked but for my stilettos, and he doesn't hesitate to move forward and press himself flush against me.

One hand slips into my hair while the other grips my throat and his mouth descends on mine, savaging me as though he has lost control.

I match his fierceness and find my leg lifting around his waist so I can get the friction I need.

His hand leaves my throat and splays across my clavicle before sliding down to caress my breast. His fingers find my nipple, pinching and rolling it until a shudder runs through my body.

Then his hand is moving again, sliding lower. Lower. *Lower.*

"You're so fucking wet." He groans against my mouth. His finger teases through my slit, circling my clit, round and round, causing me to buck against it, chasing more pressure.

"Jesus *Christ.*" His mouth leaves mine and he roughly turns me around and places a hand on my back, pushing me forward.

I'm bent over and my hands find purchase on the glass in front of me as I desperately try to stay on my feet.

He leans down, his body covering my own and it feels overwhelming and too much, but even as I think that, I find my ass pushing back, demanding more.

"Does anyone else have a key to this room?" His

harsh voice breaks the silence and his question sobers me momentarily.

"I don't think so."

"Good enough." I feel that smirk, the one I am beginning to love so much, against my back before his lips begin to kiss their way down my spine.

There is a final kiss to my right ass cheek and then he's gone. All contact broken. I glance up at his reflection in the window and I watch him. The only sound in the room is my labored breathing and the clinking of his belt buckle. I close my eyes and let the anticipation consume me.

The sound of his zipper lowering causes a painful ache to pulse through my pussy. Wetness slips down my thighs, and when I hear the rip of foil, I am ready to beg for his cock. His hand lands on my hip, his grip so tight I'm sure he will leave marks and I find myself enjoying the idea.

"Chicago?" His voice startles me and I look up to meet his gaze in the window. "You ready?" Before I can respond, he thrusts forward, seating himself deep within me, and an unflattering grunt quickly morphs into a long moan of pleasure.

Wrapping an arm across my chest he pulls me upright and presses me against the window. The glass is cold against my heated skin and I look down to see the lights of the traffic. I imagine strangers in the cars below looking up and spotting the lewd image of me, pushed up against the transparent surface getting fucked from behind.

"You're fucking perfect, Charlie." Miles pulls out and pushes back in, both hands now locked on my hips.

"So good. So, so, so good. Harder, *please*." My voice is barely a whisper, but his strokes pick up speed, and when I slip my fingers to my clit and start rubbing, I feel my orgasm start to build.

He's rutting into me with what feels like feral desperation, and when his soft grunts start to come faster, my fingers gather speed and I come with a ferocity I have never felt before.

Moments later, Miles pushes himself deep within me, and with my name a strangled whisper on his lips, he comes forcefully and emphatically.

The air in the room is heavy with the scent of sex and I don't remember ever being so sated. I also don't remember ever being fucked so thoroughly, so there's that.

We take a moment, our breathing still coming fast, and his hands are gently caressing my skin. I'm enjoying the intimacy of this moment almost as much as the sex itself.

"That was unexpected." Miles' voice is rough, as though he has been yelling. Oh God, I hope we weren't yelling.

"Really?" I challenge. "I'm not sure that was entirely unexpected on your part."

"It was definitely unexpected. A guy can dream, Chicago, but they rarely come true." He kisses my shoulder and chuckles. "You're one to talk anyway. No bra or panties? I think you were planning on seducing me tonight."

"Hmm… I may have had some plans," I tease.

He pulls out of me and the loss hits me immediately.

"Let me get rid of the condom and I'll be right back." I turn to see him head for the bathroom. Still fully dressed, I note, while I'm standing here stark naked in stilettos.

I bend down and grab my dress, slipping it back on just as he returns.

"Here, let me help." He gently turns me and starts pulling the zipper up. "Even if it does hurt my heart to cover up this body. You should be naked all the time. Have you ever considered living in a nudist community? I would highly support that decision." He's buttoning his shirt and I can't help but feel disappointed that I didn't get to see more of him.

"You would, huh?"

The sound of the hotel room door beeping surprises both of us and I look up to see Dean Ellis, another junior associate of the firm, walk in.

"Charlotte? Kendall sent me up to make sure everything was okay with the contract?" Dean's eyes are glued to his phone screen and I'm not sure he has even noticed that Miles is in the room.

"Yes, everything is fine. It took me a while to find it, it was buried under a pile of files." I'm surprised how smooth my voice is, the lie rolling off my tongue easily.

"Okay, good." He glances up and notices Miles, giving him one of those head tilt things men are so fond of. "Hey, man." He turns back to me. "Kendall's on the warpath, apparently Brennan is trying to pull some kind of shady deal, so she wants us all back here at eight tomorrow, not eleven."

"Great." I groan, my plan for sleeping in evaporating.

"I know, right. Look, I'm going to take off for the night, I'll catch you tomorrow." Another head tilt thingy directed at Miles and Dean is gone.

I collapse into a fit of giggles, the fear of how close we came to being caught sending a burst of adrenaline through me.

"Jesus, that was close." Miles runs a hand through his unkempt hair.

"*Too* close." I snigger. "Fortunately, Dean is notoriously self-centered, so I doubt he noticed anything untoward."

Miles walks toward me, an evil glint in his eye, and pulls me to him. "In that case, how about another round?"

I laugh, enjoying the ease between us, and push him away. "Nice try, Kent. Let's go."

This time it's my turn to drag him behind me, but he follows dutifully, only grumbling a little.

He has just pressed the button to the lobby when he looks at me quizzically. "I never did ask, why are you guys working in a hotel, instead of your office?"

"Oh, this Brennan guy is a complete asshole." I shake my head in annoyance. "He insisted on working all weekend to finalize this deal we're working on, but he refused to come into the office. So here we are." I shrug.

"He sounds like a peach."

I sigh sadly. "I wish I could say he's the exception but, sadly, he's not."

Miles pulls me closer and wraps his arms around me. "I'm sorry you have to deal with that."

The elevator doors open, revealing the lobby, and we step out. We're about to head back to the ballroom when a voice calling my name stops me. I turn around and see Tiff Klein looking at me impatiently.

I give Miles an apologetic smile. "Can you give me a minute? I'll meet you at the bar."

"Sure thing." Miles looks nonplussed and gives me a quick kiss on my neck.

I take a moment to watch him walk away before I go over and greet Tiff.

"Mrs. Klein, how can I help you?"

"Look, I just thought I would give you a little warning, woman to woman," she starts, her voice icy. "That man is trouble. He's a known liar and is completely untrustworthy. I like you, Charlotte. You're a smart woman and you need to get rid of him before he destroys your life. Just ask Aspen Teller what that feels like." She raises a perfectly plucked brow at me and then without another word, stalks off in the same direction Miles took.

I play her words over in my mind, stunned, but there is really only one statement that I'm concerned with at the moment.

Who the hell is Aspen Teller?

CHAPTER TWELVE

MILES

"You did what?"

"Where?"

Camden's and Shannon's incredulous voices overlap each other as they stare at me with very different expressions. My best friend wears a look of proud approval, while his wife looks slightly confused.

It's the day after the night before. The night of mind-blowing hotel sex. The night I realized exactly how far out of my league Charlie actually is.

I glance around their backyard, ensuring there are no little ears close by, but Lulu, Tyson, and Brianna are too busy chasing the dog to be bothered by what we are talking about.

"You heard me. I'm not repeating myself." I glare at the both of them.

"I would high five you right now if my wife wasn't sitting right there." Cam smirks at me.

"Wait, I thought you were serious about this woman?" Shannon's brows dip and she appraises me thoughtfully. "I mean fucking a girl at her work party doesn't scream serious to me." Camden opens his mouth to say something, but Shannon shoots a hard stare at him, and he makes the smart choice to keep quiet.

"No, it's definitely serious. I just don't have any self-control when it comes to her," I admit with an unapologetic shrug. "She has her shit together, you know? She always seems so composed and a little guarded, but when she's with me, it's as though she trusts me enough to let loose, and that drives me fucking crazy. I want to push her boundaries and see her let go, knowing that's a part of her only I get to see." I take a gulp of coffee and since Cam and Shannon aren't saying anything I plow on, because talking about Charlie is becoming one of my favorite things to do.

"There's just, there's something so authentic about her. She's kind of awkward and there is something slightly innocent about her, like she doesn't quite know how to navigate this thing between us. Sometimes she goes completely silent on me, but I know it's because she's trying to find the exact perfect thing to say or she's overthinking something *I* said and instead of frustrating me, it fucking *thrills* me because I know it means she cares about what's happening between us." I pause, inhaling deeply, and continue. "Then I saw her last night, and she seriously blew my mind. She was confident and so fucking smart. People were hanging on her every word and I had no idea what she was talking about half the time, but I *want* to. I want to listen to her explain the complexity of acquiring a company, or the intricacies of drafting contracts for multimillion-dollar deals." I shake my head. "Every boring-as-fuck detail, I want to hear it."

I look up to find the two of them staring at me, their mouths slightly agape. Shannon's eyes are bright, and she looks like she wants to jump up and tackle hug me, but Camden's hand on her thigh holds her still.

"We're happy for you, man, you deserve this."

Shannon nods in agreement. "And she knows about the show?"

I ignore the twist of my gut. "I told her about it."

"You told her everything?" Her voice holds a note of disbelief that intensifies my discomfort.

"There's something you need to know."

A shadow of wariness slips across her face and I can see her physically brace herself for bad news.

"Okay." She tries to give me an encouraging smile, but it comes out as more of a grimace.

I have no idea how to do this, so I decide to just rip off the Band-Aid.

"I was on a reality TV show last year." My hands grip my empty glass and I watch my knuckles turn white dispassionately.

"Oh." I drag my gaze across to her and she looks surprised, but relieved. "That must have been fun?" She sounds uncertain. "What kind of show?"

"It was a dating show." I watch as the relief transforms into hesitation.

"You said you're single." Her words are sharp and there's a subtle undertone of accusation.

"I am." I rush to reassure her, determined to drive the

hurt from her eyes. "I promise you I am one hundred percent single."

She still looks doubtful and I consider how much I need to tell her and how much I can, in good conscience, keep to myself.

"They pitched the concept to me as a social experiment. They would do all sorts of testing on me and the women to make sure I was matched with people who I was compatible with and who would make a good partner." I glance at her to make sure she's still invested and I'm relieved to find her listening intently.

"It was only half true. I went through all kinds of testing. Psychological, personality, even this pheromone test that I really don't want to re-live." Her nose wrinkles in distaste. "I found out later that the women they matched me with never did any of the testing. There were a few genuine people on the show, but the majority were models and actresses who were just trying to get their face on television." I grit my teeth and then force myself to go on. "It was a giant shit show and I'm still dealing with the fallout now. I regret ever agreeing to do it and I would hate for it to change your opinion of me."

I slump down in my chair and wait.

Charlie's eyes are bouncing around the shop and I can see that she's processing everything I've just told her. I give her the silence she needs and hope my mistake isn't going to ruin what we have started to build.

"You're definitely single?"

"Yes."

"Then I think that's all I need to know." Her voice leaves

no room for argument, which is good because I have no interest in fighting her.

"I'll take that as a no." Shannon's voice is droll.

"I told Charlie the basics, the important stuff," I answer defensively.

"No, you told her what you wanted her to know."

"The other stuff isn't true— oomph." Lulu body-slams onto my lap, her head narrowly missing my junk.

"Daddy." She peeks up at me and for a moment she looks so much like Renee it shocks me. Then I blink and it's gone.

"What's up, Lu?"

"Can she come to the pengwins with us?" Her little hand reaches out to snatch a strawberry from the fruit platter Shannon put out for all of us, and she shoves it in her mouth.

"Chew with your mouth closed, please." I wait for her to finish. "Can who come with us?"

"Charlie. *Jesus.*" The contrast between the harsh cuss and her childish voice is jarring and she rolls her eyes at me like she's a sixteen-year-old trapped in a two-year-old body.

"Language, Tallulah," I chastise her, doing my best to ignore Camden and Shannon, who are trying to hold in their laughter.

"Can she?" Lulu ignores my reprimand.

"I don't think so, kid, Charlie has to work today."

She groans loudly and dramatically and, not for the first time, I pray for future me.

"You like her, huh?"

"I like her bracelet." She tilts her head to the side. "She has pretty hair."

I lift her up to sit on my lap properly and agree. "Yeah, she does."

Out of the corner of my eye, I notice Cam making a gagging gesture and take great satisfaction when Shannon slaps him across the stomach and he doubles over.

"I'll ask her. If she finishes work in time, she *might* be able to join us, but no promises, okay?"

"'Kay." She jumps off my lap and races back to join Tyson and Brianna, who are now inside, engrossed in an episode of *Dora the Explorer*.

"I can't believe she already met Lulu. You never let the women you're dating meet her." Camden leans down and grabs a chunk of pineapple, while Shannon nods in agreement.

"I mean it wasn't planned, but I'm glad it happened. I'm pretty sure the kid thing freaked her out a bit, but I really think that night helped ease her mind."

"Miles, you need to tell her the whole truth about the show," Shannon presses. "I think it's great that you've met someone you feel so strongly about, but if you want things to keep going well you need to be completely honest." She leans forward, concern etched on her face. "I know it's all bullshit, but if she finds out and you're not the one to tell her, she's going to want to know why. More likely than not, she's going to jump to the conclusion that there's some truth to it."

I know she's right. The idea of reliving that nightmare again is nauseating, but I can't risk my silence backfiring on me.

"Fine, I'll tell the next time I see her."

"Text her now." Shannon refuses to let it drop. "See if she can go to the aquarium with you guys."

"You're impossible, you know that?" I check my watch and see it's just after midday. We'll need to leave soon, and I doubt Charlie will be able to get away from work, but it won't hurt to ask.

Miles: Hey, Chicago. I know your working today but we're heading to the aquarium and I promised Lulu I'd see if you could come. Consider this your invite

Charlie: Can't, working until late.
Charlie: *You're

Her correction makes me chuckle, but it quickly stops when I notice the lack of warmth in her first message. I know she's at work, but we've been texting regularly for weeks now, and she's never normally that short.

"Everything okay?" Camden asks.

I realize Shannon has gone inside while I was messaging, and I make a note to go and check on Lulu in a minute.

"I don't know, she sounds a bit off," I admit, reluctantly.

"I wouldn't worry about it." He shrugs. "I mean, it's only been, what? Twelve hours since you last saw her?

And all she's done since then is sleep and work. She's probably just busy and doesn't have time to be sexting her DILF boyfriend." He waggles his eyebrows at me in a disturbing way.

"Yeah, I guess so." My mind is already replaying last night. After the exceptional sex, we were headed back to the ballroom when she was stopped by that woman in the lobby who I presume is a client. Charlie joined me a few minutes later and she was a bit distracted, but when I questioned her, she just rolled her eyes and made a joke about demanding clients.

I had hoped we would spend the night together, but when the party came to an end, Charlie apologized, explaining she needed to get some sleep before work today.

I wrack my brain trying to figure out what could have happened, but she seemed fine. Distracted, but fine.

"Daddy!" Lulu yells from inside. "It's pengwin time, let's go!"

Camden shakes his head, laughing. "You need to watch her, man. Every time I see her, she reminds me of Grayson a little more."

"Watch your fucking mouth." I smirk. "That's my baby girl you're comparing to a walking nightmare."

I turn to head inside. "All right, kid. Let's go see the peng*wins*."

"Hi, you've reached Charlotte Reed. Please leave a message and I'll get back to you as soon as possible. Thank you."

"Hey, uh, it's me. I just wanted to see how your day was. I got stuck watching penguins for forty-five minutes at the aquarium before Lulu got bored and demanded to come home. So, yeah, uh, that was my day. Anyway, call me when you get a chance."

I end the call with a sense of dread simmering in my gut. A feeling that I have no plausible explanation for other than instinct.

I load the dishwasher, pausing halfway through to turn on the television, flicking through the channels looking for a game. Instead, I find *Miss Congeniality* and I allow Sandy B to do her thing and cheer me up.

This is the time of day that I hate the most. After a full-on day at the clinic or with Lulu, the silence after I have put her to sleep is always so overwhelmingly loud.

I have just slumped onto the sofa, remote in hand, when my phone vibrates against my ass. I pull it out of my pocket and grin like a psycho when I see Charlie's name lit up on the screen. Quickly unlocking my screen, I open her message and the smile slips from my face.

Charlie: Busy day, not feeling good, talk soon.

Something is definitely not right here. Whether she's blowing me off or she really is sick. I'm about to get to the bottom of it. Checking the time, I wince. Dad is not a night person and this favor is going to cost me.

Miles: Can you come over and watch Lulu for me?
    Dad: Does this have something to do with your girl that you've yet to tell me about?

Jesus Christ, Grayson has a big mouth.

Miles: Yes.
    Dad: Be there in twenty.

CHAPTER THIRTEEN

CHARLOTTE

My hand hovers over the play button, and as I've done countless times during the last twenty-four hours, I start the video.

Miles fills my laptop screen, followed by a gaggle of stunning women. He's laughing as they all vie for his attention at some kind of party. The sound is off, but I have watched it enough times to know it by heart. Superficial flirting and thoughtless promises are thrown at him by vapid beauties who show more enthusiasm talking to the camera than they do him.

I'm pretty upset, so there is a chance my opinion is biased but I'm too far gone to care.

I stop the video and pull up a different one. This one features an interview with Aspen Teller. I fast-forward to the part where grainy footage of Miles pulling a girl into his room is displayed while Aspen's voice plays over it.

"I trusted him. He was telling me everything I wanted to hear, promising me the world." Her voice becomes choked up and the screen cuts back to her, sitting dignified while tears fall down her highlighted cheeks. "He told me he knew I was the woman for him from the start and it killed him to have to proceed with the show, dating those other women when he was in love with me." She looks off to the side, looking sadly lost in her thoughts. "When he didn't pick me, I was devastated. When I was told that he didn't choose Karlie either, I was shocked." She turns and looks at the interviewer who is off-screen. "But when I found out he was fucking the makeup artist throughout the entire show, I was furious."

I pause the screen, Aspen's hard expression staring back at me.

My eyes are tired and sore from all of the crying, not to mention staring at my computer, watching hours upon hours of footage from the train wreck that is *Dating the DILF*.

Nothing Aspen has said in the multitudes of interviews I have seen and read today rings true with the man I have been dating and I would have no problem disregarding everything she had said, if it wasn't for the footage.

After my encounter with Tiff Klein last night, I begged off spending the night with Miles, using work as an excuse, and as soon as I got home, I hit up Google. Google had always been my friend. Until last night.

Last night Google crushed my hopes one page of results at a time. And there were a lot of pages.

After staying up most of the night, I headed in to

work this morning, only to be sent home by Kendall, who took one look at me and assumed I was sick. Normally I would have argued, determined to work through anything in order to prove my dedication. Today I left without a fight.

Which is a slap-in-the-face reminder why I don't do relationships. Because no matter how perfect you think someone is for you, you always end up here. Curled up on your sofa, cat asleep behind you, coffee table littered with empty ice cream containers—yes, plural, don't judge me—your best boxed-wine, and used tissues, while you watch hours of footage of your boyfriend wooing other women before screwing them all over.

I mean the facts might change a little every time, but you get my gist.

I pull up a random episode of the show and press play. Miles and Karlie, the other last woman standing, are sitting in a lush garden filled with wildflowers and enjoying a picnic.

"Do you want more kids?" Karlie looks at him sweetly and takes a sip of champagne.

"Absolutely. I can't imagine only having one." He grins at her. "What about you? Are kids in your plan?"

Are kids in your plan?

No, kids were not in my plan and yet after only a few weeks of being charmed by a pretty face, I was considering a whole new future.

What is wrong with me?

"I want four," Karlie answers confidently, making those stupid flirty eyes that women make when we want to make it obvious we're interested in a guy.

"Don't get your hopes up, Karlie." I scoff at the screen. "Your future baby daddy is screwing the makeup lady behind your back."

Although is it behind her back? I mean he's running around kissing all the women on the show like his lips are about to fall off and he's trying to get in as much action as he can before it happens. And they are all talking about it and comparing notes! I mean actually discussing the nuances of Miles' technique. So, is fidelity really expected here? Is what he did with the makeup girl cheating, if there has been no clearly defined expectations between anyone?

Or am I just trying to make excuses and let him off the hook?

I slam my laptop down on the small table and grab my glass, taking a giant gulp of wine. This show hurts my head, how can anyone enjoy watching it?

Switching my wine for the ice cream, I have just shoved a huge spoonful in my mouth when my doorbell rings. I know it will be Adelaide. After texting Miles earlier, I sent her a message. Five words. **You should have told me.** I promptly turned my phone off, not wanting to hear from either of them. I should have known Addy wouldn't let it slide.

I cram another spoonful of ice cream in, then I stand, pulling my blanket tighter around my shoulders. Mintie meows at the loss of my body heat and I throw *him*—fuck Miles and his "She's a girl" bullshit—an apologetic look, before schooling my features into something more outraged for Addy's benefit.

I yank the door open. "What do you want?" I bark

out before I look up and find myself face to face with a concerned-looking Miles.

There is a moment of silence before we both talk at the same time.

"You're not Addy."

"I was worried about you."

He chuckles quietly. "No, I'm not. Are you expecting her?"

"No." My grip on the door tightens and he looks anxious, standing on my porch waiting for me to invite him in.

"You said you weren't feeling well, so I wanted to come over and see if you needed anything." He shoves his hands in his pockets and shrugs.

"Right. Yeah, I'm not. Feeling good, I mean. You should probably go." My voice is cold, and I wonder how we got here so quickly when less than twenty-four hours ago we were standing in exactly the same spot, but everything was different.

Hurt washes over his face and I avert my eyes to escape it.

"Have you been crying?" I feel his hand on my cheek before I see it coming. The warmth seeps into my skin and I want to sink into his touch so badly. I close my eyes and let myself indulge in the fantasy that today never happened, just for a second.

When I open my eyes, he is standing right in front of me, crowding me in the most wonderful way.

"You need to let me in, Chicago."

His words carry so much meaning, more than he

could possibly know, and I step back allowing him to come inside.

He moves through the entrance and into the living room and I follow dutifully, wanting to get this over with. Whatever happened before he met me shouldn't be an issue in our relationship. *Logically* I know this. But emotions aren't that straightforward and the pain I have experienced today, discovering that he might not be the person I thought he was, has made me realize that I was right. The only person you can really ever depend on is yourself and opening myself up to something more will only ever lead to heartbreak. It's the one lesson my mother taught me, and I was stupid to forget it, no matter how briefly.

I stop behind Miles and he stands there, silently surveying the shambles in front of him. I know as soon as he spots the laptop, the screen still paused on his picnic with Karlie. His back stiffens and his head drops.

"I was going to tell you."

I brush past him and flop down onto the sofa, slamming the laptop shut, and I pull Mintie onto my lap, letting his soft fur under my fingers comfort me. "You told me about the show." I shrug, desperately wanting to seem unaffected.

He walks past me and takes a seat on the other end of the sofa. Leaning forward, he places his elbows on his knees and stares straight ahead.

"You had a right to know everything, not just the part that makes me look good." He sighs and scrubs his hands over his face.

"I told you the truth. The show was a staged farce and I had no fucking clue until we were almost at the end. I kept telling them I didn't feel a connection to any of the women. That I couldn't see a future with any of them, and that was what I was there for." He looks at me and his eyes are so full of despair, his pain so visceral, it feels as though someone is crushing my chest. "I had spent the last two years trying to get over losing my best friend and trying to figure out how to do the dad thing. I felt like, like…" He shakes his head, floundering. "Like I was fucking failing at life and then suddenly out of nowhere this producer contacts me, making all these promises. I was exhausted and I had never felt so alone in my life." He visibly grimaces. "I had given up on finding someone, because who has time for that when you're working sixty hours a week and raising a child. I didn't have time to scratch my ass, let alone date."

I turn around so that I am facing him and cross my legs on the sofa. Then I wait for him to continue.

"I never slept with Sophie." He must notice my confusion because he quickly clarifies. "The makeup girl. I didn't have an affair with her. We were friends, that's all. She was the one who finally told me the truth, that the producers didn't give a fuck about me finding love and the women who I thought were there for the same reasons I was, were actually there for their own careers." He swallows harshly and I watch his Adam's apple bob with the effort. "The entire time Harvey, the producer, was nudging me toward Aspen and Karlie, telling me they were the ones the relationship experts had agreed were the best matches for me. They both seemed nice enough. I had no idea—" His lip curls in disgust. "I had no idea that they were both actresses and their job was to get me hooked while also creating all kinds of drama in the house with the other women."

"Were all of the women actresses?" I'm going through all the faces I can remember and trying to reconcile the fact that they were actually paid fakes.

"Or models. There was a handful who were genuine, but really, they shouldn't have been on the show. They were a bit unbalanced, you know? Obsessive types who were fixated on marriage. I wanted them off the show straight away, but again I was encouraged to keep them because it was good for the show. Harvey told me as long as the women I knew I wanted were around, to let them take care of who would leave the show and when. I trusted him." His voice turns bitter. "I was a jackass. I thought he was looking out for me. When Sophie finally came clean and told me the truth about the show, I felt like a fool. My dad and my brother Thomas had warned me not to do it but I had been so convinced it would be the best thing I ever did. I think I was probably delirious from exhaustion." A small smile plays across his lips. It feels like years since I last saw him smile. How is it possible it was only last night?

"Anyway, after I learned the truth, I wanted out, but Harvey threatened me with a lawsuit if I didn't continue. Filming those last few episodes was a nightmare. With the truth out, Harvey dropped all pretense that this show had anything to do with me. He told me what to say, how to act and who to pick. Aspen and Karlie were chosen to be the final two and I was supposed to choose Aspen. Instead, I chose neither and there was nothing they could do about it. I had filmed all the episodes so I had met my contract requirements, and they couldn't force me to re-shoot the final one. I walked away and went back to my life. When the show started airing, it was humiliating, but I did my best to ignore it and just roll with the punches. But then the final episode aired, and the shit hit the fan." He slumps back on the sofa and turns to look at me. "They turned me into some kind of caricature of a villain. Aspen started doing all these interviews claiming I had promised her the world when the reality was that we barely talked off camera. Then they threw Sophie under the bus and started showing all of this behind-the-scenes bullshit footage, claiming we had been sleeping together the whole time. She tried to deny it, but no one was interested in hearing it. I couldn't say anything because there is a defamation clause in my contract, and they would have sued me." His jaw clenches. "Suddenly I was on the cover of magazines and on entertainment news shows being portrayed as a cheating asshole who used the show to try and get famous. It was a fucking joke. My life had turned into a joke."

Miles scoots along the sofa, moving closer to me. "I should have told you all of this, but you need to know, I'm not that guy. Everything you saw today, none of it's real and you never need to doubt me."

I can't stop staring at him. He's wearing his truth

like a badge of honor and I *don't* doubt him. Call me stupid, but I have absolute faith in his honesty.

But that's not the point now, is it? The point is, today was a brutal reminder of the risk you have to take in every relationship. You give someone the power to decimate you and I don't know that the reward is worth the risk.

But I am not ready to say goodbye yet. I need just a few minutes more. To look at him. To listen to him. To commit him to memory before I lose him.

I reach down and grab my wine, taking a sip before offering it to Miles. He shakes his head, so I grasp the glass tightly and hold it in my lap.

"What does your family think about what happened?" It's the first question that comes to mind.

He turns slightly, settling into the sofa and making himself more comfortable. I like having him here, despite the tension in the room, and I am already dreading having to watch him walk out.

"Grayson thinks it's the funniest thing ever." A small snort escapes me as I imagine Grayson shit-stirring. "Thomas thinks it's the perfect argument against taking risks and uses it against me regularly, and my dad just likes to pretend it never happened." He shakes his head, wearing an ironic smile. "He has no idea that he's the reason I did the show in the first place."

I quirk an eyebrow. "Explain."

"My parents had the perfect relationship. They met at my mom's twenty-second birthday party and were married two months later. They had been married for twenty-nine years when we lost her, and I don't remember a day ever going by with a harsh word from either of them. They were the embodiment of what love should be and I always wanted to find what they had. After Lulu was born, it felt like I had lost my chance, so when the offer for the show came up, I jumped on it."

I'm mesmerized by his story and I wonder what it would have been like to grow up with that kind of example.

"What? You're looking at me strangely." An unsettled expression has slipped across his face.

"No, nothing. We just had very different childhoods, that's all." I offer him a small smile.

"Explain." He throws the word back at me.

"It was just me and my mom and she had a lot of boyfriends while I was growing up. Each one broke her heart." I give a sad laugh and shrug. "Your parents taught you love makes you strong, my mother showed me that love makes you weak." I hold his gaze. "I don't want to be weak."

"I don't want that either. I won't make you weak, Charlie."

He sounds so sure of himself and my chest aches painfully as my heart begs me to believe him.

"But you already did."

He glances around the disorganized room and nods once. "Right."

A heavy silence falls upon us and then Miles catches me off guard by standing abruptly. He moves in front of me and pulls me to my feet, before cupping my cheeks with his hands.

"Loving someone does make you strong, Chicago, but it's always a risk. It doesn't protect you from pain, but if you trust in your love, it *will* give you the strength to make it through anything." He lowers his forehead to mine. "I could love you, Charlie." He presses his mouth to mine and I lift my hands to grip his wrists, savoring the feel of him until he pulls away. "I believe we're worth every risk, but you need to decide if you agree." He brushes another kiss across my lips. "I hope you do."

CHAPTER FOURTEEN

MILES

I close the door behind me and lean against it, exhaling a deep breath. Seeing that laptop when I walked in, I knew I had some explaining to do but I was confident that this would be a small bump in the road, something we would talk through and move on from. But when she looked at me and declared that I made her weak, I was at a loss. As much as I want to stand my ground and demand that she give us a shot, it would be pointless.

I check the time and try to decide what to do next. I optimistically asked Dad to stay the night so I wouldn't need to rush home and I decide to head to the nearby sports bar to grab a drink.

I'm about to step away from the door when it disappears from behind me and I stumble back, Charlie's voice breathlessly calling out, "Wait!"

I have just righted myself when she throws herself into my arms, almost bowling me over.

"We're worth it," she whispers over and over until I

take her mouth in a brutal kiss, the fear of the last half hour urging us both on.

She wraps her arms around my neck and my hands slip down, grasping her ass and lifting her up so she's flush along my body. I move back into the house, kicking the door closed behind me, and head straight up the stairs. She sucks on my tongue and my cock jerks, demanding to find the heat of her pussy.

It's only a matter of moments before I stumble into her room, and needing to feel her feverish skin under my fingers, I crash us into the wall and start pulling at her sweater. She does her best to help me, but her movements are as frenzied as mine and it takes longer than it should. My mouth falls to her tits and I drag down the cup of her bra and latch on to her nipple, sucking hard. She moves against me, expelling a groan of pained pleasure that sends my hand to her other breast where I squeeze, loving the feel of her.

Her hands drop to my dick and she grips me through my jeans. It feels so fucking good I drop my head back and thrust into her hand. Letting me go, she pushes me back, drops to her feet, and immediately finishes what I started with her bra, removing it and throwing it over my shoulder.

"Can you get naked, please, Miles?"

Her voice is soft, and her polite request makes me even harder. I start to pull off my jeans, but my hands freeze when she removes her leggings and exposes her bare pussy to me.

"Do you not own any panties?" I rasp out, practically salivating at the thought of eating her out.

"They irritate me."

"Get on the bed, Chicago." Her eyes widen and she almost skips across the room and hops up on the bed where she sits with her thighs pressed tightly together.

I take a moment to watch her. She folds her arms across her stomach and the action presses her tits together making them even more prominent.

I slowly jerk my cock, enjoying the visual, and when her eyes drop to my hand and glaze over in appreciation, I decide game time is over.

"We need a condom." I work my jaw as I watch her jump up and run into the en suite bathroom, her ass jiggling.

She comes back out with a strip of foil packets and I have to bite back a laugh.

"Feeling ambitious tonight?"

She shakes her head with a smile. "I have faith in you. Don't let me down."

I stalk toward her, and all trace of humor disappears. She walks backward slowly, countering my approach, and when her knees hit the bed, her ass falls onto it making her eye level with my dick. She licks her lips, and if I didn't need to get inside her so badly, I'd open those plump, pillowy lips and shove my cock between them.

Instead, I wrap my hand around her throat and bend down to lick along the seam of her mouth. She tastes sweet, chocolate and mint lingering on her skin, a combination I will forever associate with her.

I push her back and a soft gasp sounds when her back meets the mattress. I crawl up along her body, enjoying the sensation of her skin against mine. When my mouth finds hers, I nibble along her bottom lip before looking her in the eye. "Hi."

"Hey," she whispers, and the sound of her voice so close to my ear and the feel of her breasts pressed against me sends my heart slamming into my chest.

"You want to do the honors?" Her brow crinkles until I hand her one of the foil packets.

She snatches it from me and I move to a straddle position, across her chest, and start roughly stroking myself. She quickly rips open the packet and then her tiny hands are rolling the condom down my length. She bites her lip and stares at my dick with the kind of concentration I have never seen before. When she has finished, she places a kiss on the tip and then grins up at me.

"I've never done that before." The pride in her voice makes me laugh, but when she gently squeezes me, my laugh quickly becomes a groan.

I settle myself between her legs, and just like last night, my need for her makes it impossible to take this slow and I thrust into her forcefully. She wraps her legs around my waist, her feet drawing me closer as she meets me thrust for thrust.

The room fills with the sound of skin slapping against skin and Charlie's moans become louder the faster I pound into her. I duck my head down and take her nipple between my teeth, pulling roughly with every drive forward. Her hands thread through my hair and she drags me back up until our mouths come together, a mess of tongue and teeth. I swallow each of her moans, telling her how good she feels, and when she presses her head back into the mattress, her eyes squeezing shut and her pussy chokes my dick, I lose control. Relentlessly, I slam into her, chasing my own orgasm. When it comes, I bury myself inside her as deep as I can get, grunting out my release before falling on top of her.

She taps my back and mumbles something against my chest forcing me to roll off her.

"Sorry about that."

"You have nothing to apologize for. That was totally worth a little suffocation." She grins at me, her eyes glinting wickedly.

"Give me a sec." I jog to the bathroom and get rid of the condom, hurrying back to Charlie.

She curls into my side and kisses my shoulder. "I need to say something."

"Okay." A wisp of dread curling in my gut.

"You lied to me." I start to deny it, but she cuts me off. "Not an outright lie, but a lie of omission. You *knew* what you left out of the story was important and something I should have been told and you need to know I won't be so forgiving next time." She tilts her head back to look me in the eye. "So, don't do it again."

"I won't." I roll to my side so we're lying face to face. I let my eyes drop to admire her tits briefly before moving back to her face. "I thought we were over."

"So did I." Her confession hurts. "But I heard what you said, and when I watched you walk out, I realized that I was losing you because I was too scared to risk losing you, which is just ridiculous." She shakes her head.

"You can trust me." I lean forward and brush my nose against hers. "I promise we'll figure it all out."

"I know," she whispers. "Wait, where's Lulu?"

"My dad is spending the night at my place."

"The whole night, huh?"

I wrap my arm around her and drag her closer. "The whole night."

"Hmmm… what could we do with all that time— Oh God." Her drawn-out cry is the last thing I hear before her thighs clamp around my ears.

"Do you have a 'gina?" Lulu's question breaks the silence that had been lingering while we eat our food. I quickly glance at Charlie who is looking slightly horrified and I wonder just how much she is regretting accepting my dinner invitation.

Charlie takes a deep breath and lays her cutlery flat on her plate. "Yes."

"'Cause you're a girl." Lulu nods knowingly. "My dad has a penis 'cause he's a boy."

"Yes, he does."

I smirk at her across the table, considering all the ways she has become acquainted with my penis over the last few weeks.

"But I'm a girl like you, so I have a 'gina."

"Lulu." I clear my throat. "The dinner table isn't an appropriate time for this conversation."

"'Kay." She turns back to Charlie. "He says that a lot."

"Really?" She quirks a brow at me. "Because I have the opposite problem with your dad." I chuckle at her pointed expression but Lulu just groans.

"I'm done." She pushes her plate away, which still has a taco sitting on it, untouched. "Can I watch TV?"

I consider trying to get her to finish her meal, but I don't really feel like an argument, so I let it slide. "Twenty minutes," I tell her and she bounces out of her seat and races to her playroom.

"She likes you."

"She terrifies me," Charlie admits, like it's a huge secret. "But it feels like a good kind of terror. I don't think I've ever wanted to impress someone so much before." She shakes her head.

"Well, consider her impressed." I stand up and start to gather our plates.

Charlie follows me into the kitchen and hops up to sit on the countertop while I load the dishwasher and I pause for a moment to appreciate the way her skirt rides up a little higher on her thighs.

"I settled the Morrison Inc. lawsuit today." She beams at me and I straighten, moving in between her legs, grabbing her ass and sliding her to me.

"That's fucking amazing." I take her mouth in a kiss and she wraps her legs around my waist. "I'm proud of you."

She ducks her head, a perfect pink blush staining her cheeks.

"Anyway, it means I can take the weekend off and I

thought maybe we could do something together. The three of us, I mean." She presses her hands to my chest and kisses my chin. "Only if you want to, though. I know we're taking it slow with Lulu, I just thought…" Her voice trails off, unsure.

It has been tough navigating this new relationship. I want to do the right thing by both Lulu and Charlie, and I've felt a lot of pressure to help them start to build a relationship in a way that doesn't make Lulu feel like she's being replaced as the most important person in my life.

But Lulu has accepted Charlie, without question, every time she has seen her and has even started bringing her up when she's not around.

Maybe I need to just follow Lulu's lead, and as long as she's happy, go with the flow?

"That sounds great." I tighten my arms around her waist. "Gray and I were actually planning on taking Lulu to the hockey game on Saturday, you should come. Invite Addy too." I congratulate myself. I get a day with my girls and Grayson will owe me for getting him time with Adelaide.

"I've never been to a hockey game."

I push away slightly and look at her with shock. "You've never been to a hockey game?"

She shakes her head.

"Then you have to come. Besides, I need all the backup I can get."

"Why's that?"

"It's a Blackhawks–Penguins game. Lulu supports the Penguins. *Loudly.*" I cringe remembering our last game and all the dirty looks we got. "The Blackhawks supporters don't really appreciate it."

"Hmph, well, I've got her back." She laughs.

I'm about to go in for another kiss, when my phone shrills loudly. I pull it out of my pocket and all the blood rushes from my face when I see the name Sophie lit up. Sophie and I haven't spoken in months. We decided it was best to cut off all contact, when a "friend" of hers revealed to a tabloid we were still in touch.

Charlie's surprised expression mirrors my own and I answer the phone with trepidation.

"Hey, Soph."

"Miles, shit is about to hit the fan."

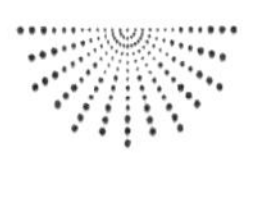

CHAPTER FIFTEEN

"Oh, hell no," Gray barks.

"Pengwins!" Lulu cheers.

"It's good to see you again too, Grayson." I lean down on Miles' car and peer in through the window, Miles sniggering behind me. "Hey, Lulu."

"No. No, no, no, no, no, *no*. I'll put up with it from her." He points to Lulu who is sitting innocently in her car seat beside him. "But not you. You're a grown-ass woman, Charlie, you should know better."

"Grown-ass woman!" Lulu laughs.

I look down at my outfit. "What exactly do you object to?"

"Uh, the Penguins jersey. Obviously." He sticks his head out the window and points at Miles. "Tell her she can't get in the car wearing that."

"Not a chance in hell." He comes up behind me and kisses my neck.

Addy pushes past us both, groaning. "No PDA,

please. Sharing a confined space with Grayson has me feeling nauseous enough, thank you very much."

She rounds the car, an annoyed look on her face.

"I may have accidentally on purpose forgotten to mention that Grayson was coming." I pull a face.

"Meh, they'll live. Now, get in the car, woman." He smacks my ass and I shoot a glare his way. "Please," he quickly adds.

The drive to the arena isn't far from my downtown townhouse and Grayson has me in stitches the entire time. He's trying so hard to impress Addy and she is not giving him an inch. It's also nice to see Miles so relaxed. He's been on edge all week, since Sophie's call.

I have to say, while I appreciate the sentiment behind the warning, I almost wish she hadn't bothered. There was nothing she could tell him other than she had heard "whisperings." They both seem to think this producer, who sounds like a complete slimeball if you ask me, is going to try to find a way to sue Miles for breach of contract for failing to appear on the reunion show. I've scoured his contract and assured him that he would have no cause. The contract contains no mention of any appearance other than the *Dating the DILF* television series. Any reunion shows, or spin-offs, would have had to have been specified for it to hold up in a court of law.

"Lulu, hold my hand." Miles tries to get a grip on her hand as we all get out of the car, but Lulu snatches it away.

"No, I hold Charlie's hand." Her little voice is so

firm, and she grabs my hand before I can object, holding on with a strong grip.

A wave of something good washes over me, until I look up and see the thousands of people rushing into the arena and panic seizes me. I squeeze her hand tighter, determined not to lose her.

"Princess, hold my hand."

"Grayson, eat my—"

"Adelaide!" I cut her off with a scowl. She looks down at Lulu contritely.

"Sorry, the kid thing is going to take a little getting used to."

She's telling me. Lulu walked into the kitchen the other night when my ass was planted on the counter, my legs wrapped around her daddy's waist and I was practically eating his face. I pushed him away so fast and hard he almost fell flat on his ass.

Lulu acted as though it was nothing out of the ordinary and Miles almost bust a gut laughing. I, however, was mortified.

We head into the giant arena and the scale of it overwhelms me. It's huge and it's filled with people heading in every direction. I'm not much for crowds and a hockey game would normally be a hard pass for me, but Miles was so excited, and I couldn't deny I wanted to spend some more time with Lulu. She kind of reminds me of Mintie. I was happily living my life without a clue that she existed but, suddenly, through a random twist of fate, I have a cat in my life, and I find myself liking it.

Is it poor form to compare a child to an animal? Oh well, they're both cute as a button, I'm sure it's fine.

Thirty minutes later, we're all in our seats, loaded down with hot dogs, pretzels, and popcorn waiting for the game to start. The air is practically vibrating with anticipation and, even though I know nothing about hockey, I find the excitement is contagious.

Lulu, in her Penguins jersey, is getting many indulgent looks. I, however, am not faring so well. My jersey is garnering me a lot of dirty glares and I'm beginning to second-guess my decision to show solidarity with Lulu.

I'm sandwiched between Miles and Addy, and when Miles is distracted, helping Lulu with her hot dog, Addy nudges my shoulder.

"Let's do a bathroom run before the game starts."

I agree, and after letting the boys know where we're headed, we go in search of the closest restroom.

We find it easily, stunned to find it empty which, let's face it, is the female equivalent to winning the lottery.

"So," Addy calls out from the stall. "You and Miles are sickening together, I hope you know that."

"I do." I stand at the sink, washing my hands and grin at my reflection. Every day I'm a little less surprised at how easily my smiles are coming.

The sound of the toilet flushing echoes through the room and Addy comes out, rolling her eyes at my expression.

"I honestly didn't think you'd stick it out. I'm proud of you, Charlie." She starts scrubbing her hands. "I was convinced you would run for the hills after seeing the show."

"Well, maybe if I'd been more prepared it wouldn't have been such a surprise." I shoot a quick frown her way. I still haven't totally forgiven her for that.

"Oh, please. You were looking for a reason to run. If I had told you about it, you never would have given him a chance." She snatches some paper towels from the dispenser. "Those extra couple of weeks are the reason you were invested enough to stick with him when you found out. *You're welcome.*" She tosses the towels in the trash and I start to head for the door when she stops me.

"Wait, I have a question to ask you."

"Yes, you should go out with Grayson."

She purses her lips and scowls. "Never gonna happen so move on." She pauses and takes a deep breath. "So, before the show aired, Miles did a photoshoot for a magazine and he was wearing only a towel."

I bite my lip, the memory of Miles telling me his embarrassment over that shoot vivid in my mind.

"Okay, look, there's no polite way to ask this so I'm just going to do it. Is your boyfriend hung, because you could see the outline through that towel and it definitely *looked* like he was hung." She pauses and I just stare at her, completely flummoxed. "Is he a big-dick Bruce, or not?" she finally spits out.

"Big-dick Bruce?" I repeat the phrase slowly, sure I misheard.

"Yeah, like Bruce Willis."

"Bruce Willis has a big dick?" I ask, confused.

"I mean, I think he would, don't you?"

"I— I had never thought about it."

"Well?" she prompts and I burst out laughing.

"You are such an inappropriate human."

"This is not news," she replies ruefully.

"Uh, well, I mean it's not anaconda-style, run-from-the-room *huge*, but it's definitely bigger than any other dick I've encountered before, and I am slightly concerned for my jaw when I finally blow him."

"You haven't blown him yet?"

"Oh my God, *go!*" I push her toward the door.

"Fine, but I'd just like to say you're a shitty friend for forcing me to ask the question. A real friend would have given me all the details as soon as you slept with him."

Pushing her through the door, I bite my lip to hide my grin.

When we reach our seats again there has been some movement and Grayson is now sitting beside the aisle, leaving two vacant seats, then Lulu, then Miles, who shoots us an apologetic smile.

"He threatened to never babysit again."

Addy huffs and flops down into the chair next to Lulu, but she is not having any of that.

"No, you move," Lulu growls at Addy. "That's Charlie's seat."

"You're killing me, kid." Adelaide groans.

Lulu just points to the other chair. "Move!"

Two hours later, I am laughing hysterically at Lulu's antics as she riles up all the Chicago fans around us, cheering on her Penguins loudly and proudly. I understand what Miles was talking about now, realizing all the indulgent looks from earlier have transformed into glares of annoyance. Especially since the score is not in their favor.

On my other side, Adelaide and Grayson have been bickering nonstop. While Grayson looks like he's having the time of his life, Addy looks ready to kill.

Him, me, I'm not sure she's overly concerned with the details.

Something happens down on the ice, which I miss. This isn't overly surprising since I haven't spent much time watching the actual game. Everyone around me jumps to their feet yelling and it's only when they all start to quiet down and take their seats again that I see one of the Pittsburgh players heading for the penalty box.

Lulu must notice at the same time because the next thing I hear is her voice yelling at the top of her lungs, *"Jesus Christ, Karen!"*

It feels like everyone in our vicinity has turned to stare while Miles quietly chastises her. When an older gentleman in front of us turns his judgemental stare my way, my usual timidity deserts me and I roll my eyes. "Oh, please. Who *doesn't* love a good Karen joke?"

Down below us one of the coaches calls a time-out and immediately the giant screen above the ice starts showing the crowd. The camera pans across until it lands on a couple in the stands, a loveheart surrounding them on screen and the words *kiss cam* flashing.

To my right, Grayson starts loudly cheering and he turns to Addy with a huge grin. "Pucker up, baby, the camera can't resist this face."

Adelaide turns to me with a panicked look. "Switch seats with me." I shake my head laughing and cross my fingers that Gray gets his wish. I am totally shipping *Graddy*.

"Daddy!" I look across at Lulu who is pointing at the screen and waving. When I look up, I find my own wide eyes staring back at me, a bemused Miles by my side, the two of us surrounded by a red heart.

"Kiss her, asswipe," Gray yells across Addy's chest before resting his head on her breasts with a blissful grin. She smacks him and pushes him off.

"Kiss her, asswipe!" I can't control my laughter when Lulu copies Grayson and yells at Miles excitedly.

When he turns to look at me, the expression he's wearing is almost predatory, and before I have a chance to object, his hand grips my neck and drags me to him. His mouth finds mine in a passionate and all too brief kiss, before he pulls back slightly and gently runs his thumb across my bottom lip.

The sound of cheering and hollering draws our attention back to the big screen and my exuberance over the moment vanishes when I see that now, instead of reading *kiss cam*, the screen declares itself *DILF cam*, and a sense of dread twists deep in my stomach.

CHAPTER SIXTEEN

"Those *fuckers.*"

"Are you really surprised?" Sophie's husky voice travels through the car speakers.

"Not at all," I begrudgingly admit. "To be honest, we had our suspicions."

"From what I've heard, Harvey thinks if he makes enough trouble for Charlie, you'll come knocking on his door begging to defend her honor."

I swallow down a bitter laugh, because that's exactly what I had been itching to do. The second our kiss cam picture had been splashed over the tabloids with all kinds of fun headlines (my personal favorite was *Dating the Douche*) and cruel insinuations, I had wanted to get in front of any camera, any microphone, *anything*, and reveal that show for the utter garbage it was. Fuck the defamation clause.

"Hold up, Soph. I'm just pulling up to Charlie's." I see Charlie standing out in front of her house. When her face lights up with that goddamn beautiful smile and she jogs to my car, a painful ache tugs at my chest. For the first time, I'm starting to understand her fear and grasp the reality of the risk we're both taking. It was so easy for me to tell her love was worth the risk —*we* were worth the risk—when I didn't fully comprehend what it could cost us. I thought I did. I thought I had been in love before and weathered heartbreak, but I had no fucking clue what it meant to love a woman until her. If she decides this is all too much and she hands my heart back to me, an unremarkable, fragmented shell because that's all that would be left, how could I possibly come out of that still standing?

"Hey, babe." She climbs into the car and leans over to press her lush mouth to mine.

"Sophie's on speaker." I nod toward the Bluetooth display.

"Oh. Hi, Sophie," she squeaks, shooting me a nervous look.

"I was just about to tell Miles that I heard Harvey is going to hire an investigator to dig into your background."

"He won't find anything." She laughs. "I'm the most boring person alive."

"Sophie, we have to go. Thanks for the warning, I appreciate it." I end the conversation, needing to talk to Charlie alone.

"No problem. Good luck, you guys. Just ride it out, okay? There will be a new scandal soon enough, I'm sure."

We say our goodbyes and an uncomfortable silence hangs over us.

"You're worried? About the investigator?"

I glance at her quickly before turning back to the road in front of me. "A little. You're not?"

"I mean, no, not really. I wasn't joking, there is literally nothing they could use against either of us."

"What about your mom?" I ask quietly.

She flinches and quickly turns away from me to look at the passing scenery.

"She's a mess but nothing too out of the ordinary. She has a gambling problem and mooches off her boyfriends, but she's never had any trouble with the law or anything. My grandparents always made sure of that." She turns back to me wearing a forced smile. "Even if they do find something, it's just like Sophie said. There will be some new controversy rocking the world soon enough and they'll forget all about you."

I can't hide my grimace. "I've been planning on that for almost a year and yet, here we are." I reach over and squeeze her thigh. "I hate that you're going through this because of me."

"It's fine. Yes, I could do without having my picture taken as I leave the gym and finding it plastered all over the internet but—"

"They did that?" I bark.

"Not my best moment." She giggles. "But apparently a girl needs to keep her figure trim when she's coming between a true love like yours and Aspen's." I roll my eyes at her. "Seriously, I can deal with it." She lifts my hand off her thigh and threads her fingers between mine. "You're worth it, Miles. I don't think you have any idea how worth it you are." She brings our hands up to her mouth and kisses my fingers.

"Now, enough of this. I have been freaking out about this dinner all week. That is the issue we need to be focusing on."

"Why are you freaking out?" I don't try to hide my amusement. "You've spoken to my dad on the phone and he already loves you more than me. You've met Gray. There's nothing to be worried about."

"God, you sound so sure, I want to punch you." She drops my hand with a sigh of exasperation. "I want them all to like me. I don't make a very good first impression."

"They'll love you," I insist but she just levels me with another glare. "C'mon, I saw you at your work thing, you had them eating out of the palm of your hand."

"That was work, Miles. Is your dad going to ask me how to file a government report? Is Thomas going to ask me about the key rules for negotiating an employee contract? No." She shakes her head vehemently. "They're going to ask me things like where I grew up, which *sounds* like a very simple question, but ten minutes later when I'm rambling about the time I fell and twisted my ankle because my poppa's car had broken down so I was running for the subway, they're going to think I'm a nutcase!"

"Rambling like that, you mean?" I side-eye her with a huge grin, but her stony expression tells me she doesn't find the humor in the situation. "Well, prepare thyself, Chicago, because we're here." I pull into my dad's driveway, behind Thomas' SUV and cut the engine. "You ready?"

Her face is ashen and there are tiny little beads of sweat along her hairline. I would laugh but I'm pretty sure the punch comment wasn't an empty threat.

I lean over and grip her neck, running my thumb along her jaw. "You have nothing to worry about. We're going to go in and eat some good food, have some laughs and that's it." I want to taste her, but I know if I start I won't be able to stop, so instead, I place a gentle kiss on her upturned nose. "Now, let's go."

We walk to the front door of my dad's bungalow, and Charlie exclaims over how cute the place is. I try to look at it through her eyes, but to me, it's just home. No matter where I live, this place will always feel like coming home.

I open the door and the smell of my dad's taco casserole is like a punch in the face. It's the only dish he knows how to make, and he only brings it out when he's keen to impress.

"Wait." Charlie pulls me to a stop and looks at me panicked. "Your dad is Robert, brother is Thomas and his wife is Chrissy. What are their kids' names again? Taylor?" She's clenching my hand hard and I wonder if she might pass out.

"Tully, Carson, and Shae. You need to relax." I pull her into a hug, enjoying the way her head fits right under my chin, and bury my nose in her coconut-scented hair. "No one is going to care if you forget their name."

"Is that you, Miles?" we hear my dad shout. "Get

your ass back here, your daughter's refusing to put her clothes on."

"See." I pull back. "Forgetting a name is the least of our worries."

❧

"Hey, Gray," I shout across the table. A second later a hand is thrust over my mouth and Lulu, who has planted her ass on Charlie's lap most of the night, glowers at me.

"Don't yell, Daddy. *Christ.*"

Jesus Christ indeed.

I stare at her dumbfounded, trying to decide if I should remind her, *again*, about appropriate language. Charlie makes the decision for me, quietly whispering in her ear and handing her another cannoli to eat.

"What's up, douche?" Gray smirks at me across the table.

"I'm going to be near your work on Monday, you want to meet for lunch?"

"Sure. Downtown Pizza?" He shoves a pastry in his mouth. "Oh, wait, Monday? Yeah, I can't."

"Why not?" Grayson never turns down pizza, especially since he knows I always pick up the tab.

"Just can't, don't be such a nosey Nellie." He turns to Chrissy and asks her to pass the plate of eclairs.

"What does Grayson do?" Charlie whispers in my ear.

"He's a sports rehabilitation therapist. He works for one of the junior hockey league teams."

"Oh wow." She looks shocked, which is a fairly common response when people find out what he does *after* they've met him. "That's such a serious job. I kind of assumed he…" She trails off, her nose wrinkled cutely. "Actually, I have no idea what I thought he did."

"Hey, Nugget," Gray bellows, earning him a look of reprisal from Lulu.

"What," she snips.

"Are you excited for your birthday party next week?"

"Yes!" She squeals, bouncing on Charlie's lap. "But it's my birthday on Wednesday so you can give me my present then, okay?"

"Whatever you say." He laughs.

"Charlotte, will you be joining us for the party?" Thomas' clipped voice cuts through the din.

"Uh, yes." She looks to me for reassurance. "I hope that's okay with everyone. I don't want to intrude."

A chorus of denials bounce around the room from Dad, Grayson, and myself, and I shoot Thomas a dirty look.

"Of course she's coming. She's my girlfriend."

He shakes his head ruefully, turning back to his dessert.

"I'm getting a Barbie Dreamhouse," Lulu declares, her voice ringing with excitement, she brings everyone's attention back to her.

"Maybe. If you behave yourself for the next four days." I snatch her last bite of cannoli and pop it in my mouth.

"Daddy!" She growls.

"You gotta be quicker, kid." I lean down and blow a raspberry on her cheek, delighting in her giggles. When I straighten, I find Charlie's eyes locked on me, lit with a heady combination of amusement and desire.

"Are you having fun?" I whisper.

"Yes. I think they like me." Her voice, also a whisper, is full of optimism. I wish I could make her understand how much more it is than simply *like*. Dad and Grayson are already prepared to walk through fire for her for no other reason than she makes Lulu and me happy.

"I think so too. They probably could have done without the twenty-minute explanation of the differences between corporate and business law, but other than that, you're doing swell." I tug a lock of her hair, savoring the flush that sweeps across her cheeks.

"God, that was bad, wasn't it?" She buries her face in Lulu's hair, drawing a giggle from her.

"They love you, relax."

"Jeez, pluck a duck, we love you." Lulu reaches up, wrapping her arms around Charlie's neck and drags her down to place a sloppy kiss on her cheek.

Watching the two of them together, blood starts rushing to my head and my right arm starts to feel numb. I'm torn between wondering if this is a stroke and wanting to agree with Lulu and tell Charlie just how much I love her.

Instead, I turn to Gray and pierce him with my most severe glare. "Stop teaching my kid coded swear words."

"No idea what you're talking about." He starts

licking cream from his fingers. "Hey, Charlie, I need you to give Adelaide a message for me."

"I am not getting involved in that mess." She shakes her head, but her lips are tilted in a small smirk.

My phone vibrates against my ass, distracting me from Gray's response, and when I see the name on the screen, I quickly excuse myself and head through the kitchen to the back yard, looking for some privacy.

Stepping out into the ink-black night, I accept the call and put the phone to my ear.

"Harvey."

"Miles, nice of you to finally take my call." His words are dripping with derision.

"I didn't have anything to say to you."

"And, now?"

"Now, we need to talk."

"Good to hear it." The creak of leather sounds through the phone, followed by the snick of a lighter. I hear him inhale, then blow out a puff of air. I can almost smell the plume of smoke I know will be floating around his pallid, moon-shaped face. "We're going to shoot a reunion show next month and you're going to be on it." The certainty in his voice has me gritting my teeth. "You're going to be contrite and tell the country how you want to make amends. How sorry you are for breaking Aspen's heart and screwing around with the makeup girl. Aspen will put on a good show, a little something for her video reel, before she forgives you. You tell us how the love of a good woman has redeemed you, you're a changed man, and then voila, your reputation is absolved, and you can go back to living your life."

"You're an asshole," I grit out doing my best to control my temper.

"That may very well be true, but I'm also great at what I do, Miles, and if you want your little girlfriend's name to stop being in every tabloid in the country, you'll start toeing the line."

Charlie's words ring in my ears. Her assurance that she can cope with this, that she'll stick by me.

But for how long? How long am I willing to risk losing her, when all it will take to make it go away is a piece of my pride.

"I'll think about it." I hang up before he can answer. It's the best I can do right now.

The silence surrounds me, and I sit down next to the ancient grill that Dad refuses to get rid of, wondering how my life got so fucking complicated.

The low hum of voices in the kitchen distracts me and I stand, ready to get back to my girls, but as I get closer to the kitchen, I realize those voices belong to Thomas and Charlie and a flicker of panic surges through me.

"*Excuse me?*" Charlie's incensed tone urges me to move quicker.

"I'm just saying that it's convenient how you turned up out of nowhere and now suddenly my brother's name is being dragged through the mud all over again."

"Are you insinuating that *I'm* responsible for the trash—"

"I'm saying I'm tired of seeing my brother hurt and if I find out you're the one responsib—"

"You'll what?" I bark. "What the hell are you doing, Thomas?" The fucker doesn't even have the decency to look sorry. He merely matches my steely expression with his own.

"Someone needs to make sure—"

"*I* need to make sure, Tom. I'm the one who needs to be sure, not you. And I am. So back the fuck off and if I ever hear you talking to the woman I love like that again, we'll be sorting things out the way we did when we were kids." I grab Charlie's hand, ignoring her round eyes, and pull her behind me.

It's not until I'm sitting back at the table, the chatter of everyone around us masking my silence, that I realize what I just revealed.

CHAPTER SEVENTEEN

CHARLOTTE

I rub my eyes against the glare of my computer screen, the last few hours spent staring at the damn thing playing havoc on me. I risk another quick glance at the clock and immediately wish I hadn't.

Lulu's party started an hour ago.

I had been so sure I would make it. Determined to breeze in here at six this morning, skip yoga, power through these contracts and be at Miles' in time to help him set up for the party.

Can you say delusional?

Instead, five hours later, I am still here with more than half the contracts yet to be reviewed and summarized.

I don't know why I'm surprised. It's been the same all week. I try to concentrate but my mind is constantly distracted, too busy playing Miles' words on repeat.

If I ever hear you talking to the woman I love like that again.

I'm not sure he even realized he said it, but I haven't been able to forget. I've never had a man tell me he loves me. Hell, I don't remember the last time *anyone* told me they love me. My mother loves me in the only way she knows how, but it's not a conventional maternal love, and the only memory I have of her telling me she loved me was cocooned in an argument and thrown at me carelessly and painfully.

"I don't care if you hate me!"

"I don't hate you, Charlie, I love you. But that doesn't mean I like you."

My grandparents' love for me is enduring and consuming, but they aren't sentimental types and their love was always shown through actions, not words.

I had no idea how much I craved hearing the actual words until Miles hurled them at Thomas so nonchalantly.

God, Thomas. His accusatory glare is burned into my brain. I know he's going to fault me if I miss the party today and I hate with a passion that I'm going to feed his distrust of me.

The idea of just leaving crosses my mind, but I quickly dismiss it. I have never left a job half-finished and no matter how much I'd like to, I can't bring myself to start now.

My cell phone is lying on the corner of my desk where I tossed it after my last message to Miles, and I snatch it up, preparing myself to give him the bad news, and already trying to figure out how I will make it up to Lulu. It will definitely involve multiple gifts and multitudes of cash.

Because that's what people in my position do, right? We throw money at a problem and pray the people we love will forgive our absence, our lack of attention, our *failings*.

I have spent the last four years watching the men and women with careers I aspire to, repeating this cycle over and over again. It's how I knew children couldn't be in my future. I was determined I would never disappoint someone, casually disregarding them just as I had been over the years.

And, yet, here I am.

Sucking up every breath of defeat I feel, I start typing out an appropriately apologetic message to Miles, when I'm interrupted by a knock on my door.

Louis' distinguished face peers around my door and he offers me a quick smile.

"Charlotte, can I have a minute?" He enters my office before I can respond and takes a seat, fiddling with his tie. I instantly feel underdressed in my black skinny jeans, pink sweater, and ballet flats.

In my defense, I didn't expect to run into a partner on a Saturday.

"Charlotte, I'm going to get right to the point. We're removing you as the lawyer for Preston Pharmaceuticals."

It's funny what runs through your mind at a time like this. The moment you see your future plans crumbling down around you. The first thing that comes to mind when I hear Louis' assertion is that *Friends* quote.

"Isn't that just kick-you-in-the-crotch, spit-on-your-neck fantastic."

Internally I am wailing, howling and weeping over the unfairness of it, because how is this even possible? I busted my ass to bring that company in to Harris & Erickson, and I have been on top of my game every step of the way.

Outwardly, I maintain my composure, not skipping a beat.

"May I ask why?" My voice remains impressively calm and I want to fist-bump myself, my pride is so immense.

He sighs, and for the first time, I see a modicum of discomfort. "Unfortunately, the head of the company is uncomfortable moving forward with you as their lawyer. Considering your recent publicity." He shifts in his seat and clears his throat. "Charlotte, you have always been a credit to our firm. You're shrewd and determined, and you put in the hard hours. Honestly, both Kendall and I thought you were on the partnership track, but these last couple of months we've noticed a switch in your priorities. Normally we wouldn't comment on this, since the quality of your work has remained outstanding, but we can't ignore this tabloid business. Several clients have expressed concern regarding your commitment and possibly your ethics after reading certain things." I open my mouth to interrupt him, outraged by the suggestion that my ethics are anything less than stellar, but he cuts me off. "Please don't misunderstand. *We* are not questioning any of these things. However, having one of our attorneys presented in this negative light, well, it's not good for the firm and we need to consider our reputation above all else. I know you will understand."

"Of course," I answer soberly, waiting for him to drop the axe. I'm surprised when he simply stands and starts heading for my door.

"Excellent. Consider what I've said carefully, and I hope you make the right decision."

He's gone before the implication of his words fully hits me. When it does, I slump back in my seat.

By ending things with Miles, I can set my world right again. I'll be demonstrating my commitment to the firm and there will be no reason for clients to resist working with me. My job will be secure and my written-in-stone plan for career progression will be right back on track.

Miles and Lulu will be a tiny blip on my trajectory and one that could be overcome with hard work and sacrifice.

I worry my bottom lip between my teeth and tears prick my eyes.

The answer is obvious, so, ignoring the bile rising in my throat, I gather my things and head to Miles.

CHAPTER EIGHTEEN

CHARLOTTE

The drive only takes me twenty-five minutes, but during that time my resolution only strengthens. I know I'm doing the right thing.

I pull up to Miles' house as a group of people are leaving. Children clutching balloons and goodie bags in their sticky hands, bouncing around and giddy on a sugar high.

For a brief moment, I'm almost glad I missed the party. Almost, but not quite. Two-month-ago-me is wondering what the hell happened. Current-me pities her.

I cut the engine and hop out of the car, nausea and regret still punishing my gut over the choice I have been forced to make today, but when I glimpse Miles standing at his front door watching me, the inevitability of this soothes me.

There really is *no* other choice.

His eyes follow me, the weight of them carrying me

forward, and when I find myself standing toe to toe with him, I indulge myself, and sink into his arms.

"I'm sorry."

He chuckles against my hair, his hands threading through the loose waves and I feel his shoulders shake gently.

"Don't worry about it." He pulls back and cradles my face. "Lulu barely noticed *I* was here, let alone anyone else. She had her friends, a balloon twister, and ice cream cake, she's fine."

"I let— wait, there's ice cream cake?" I lean forward and bury my face in his chest. "Ugh, that's not important. I let her down."

He moves back, distancing himself and breaking contact. I watch him leaning on the doorframe, his eyes narrowed, scrutinizing me.

"The party is unimportant, Chicago. This—" He waves a hand behind him, motioning in the direction of childish squeals and laughter. "This is just the window dressing. The superficial show we put on. What matters is you were here when it was just us. You rearranged your schedule so you could be with us on her birthday. All those people back there, they don't matter. What they think doesn't matter. You, me, and Lulu, we're the only ones that do and you could never let us down."

In one quick motion, he pulls me to him and twists us so that I am pressed up against the wall.

"We love you, Charlie." His mouth is so close to mine, his breath ghosting across my lips. "You can't get rid of us that easy." He smiles against my mouth and then his lips take mine in a playful kiss, his tongue claiming me.

In that moment, my last shred of doubt disappears. The last two months have changed who I am and what I want out of my life. I believe with complete conviction that Miles is my future. Even if I'm wrong and I'm left heartbroken, *this* is worth the risk. This deep and genuine love that Miles has opened my heart to is new and frightening, but it's worth *everything* and I won't give it up for a job.

I place my hands on his chest and push him back lightly, giggling at his groan of frustration.

"Enough of that, take me to the child so I can beg for forgiveness."

He starts to lead me down the hallway, but I stop him, needing to acknowledge his confession and trust him with my own.

"I love you, too. Both of you." Then I push past him following the sounds of merriment. When I turn to look back at him, he's watching me, his gaze heated, and a satisfied smile plastered across his face.

"Let's go, Kent. There's ice cream cake to be eaten."

"Charlie, save me!" Lulu throws herself over my lap. "The monster's gonna get me!"

Tyson is chasing her, growling loudly, and when he reaches me, Lulu hops off and runs away screaming, peeking over her shoulder to make sure he's following.

"God, I would kill for that energy." I sigh, watching the two of them run around the yard.

"It's all about to come crashing down, just you wait." Shannon laughs.

I take a sip of my coffee and peer across at her. The last of the guests left not long after I arrived, and Shannon, Camden, and their kids are the only ones remaining. I was grateful I got the chance to see Robert and Grayson before they left, and I was even more grateful that Thomas had already gone.

The yard is empty now, except for me, Lulu, Tyson, and Shannon. Miles and Camden are inside arguing over hockey stats while Brianna plays games on her tablet. The ground out here is littered with remnants of the party and it reminds me of the way I look when I get home from a big night. A disheveled imitation of my former self, and another wave of sadness washes over me that I missed it.

"What do you mean?"

"Those two"—she points toward Lulu and Tyson —"are on a massive sugar high and they're about to crash. Trust me, it'll be our very own reality show. Toddlers, tears, and tantrums." She grins at me over the edge of her coffee mug, her blue eyes crinkling in amusement.

"I think the last thing this family needs is another reality show," I snort out, glancing across at Lulu and deciding Shannon can't be right. I haven't seen her throw a tantrum once in the time I've known her.

"I'm so glad you didn't hold that fucked-up show against him." She reaches over and places her cup on the large outdoor table that is sitting between us, swapping it for a handful of nuts. "He had good intentions, but I really don't know what he was thinking agreeing to it."

She tosses a wrapped chocolate truffle to me and I catch it easily.

"It does seem unlike him," I agree, trying to feel her out. "He doesn't come across as someone who seeks out attention like that."

"Oh, he's definitely not, but I think Ted was just feeling hopeless, you know. He was suddenly a single dad to a baby, doing it all on his own and he saw the future he had always dreamed of just slipping away."

"Ted?" I quirk a brow at her.

She laughs lightly, the melodic sound ringing through the yard. "Sorry, inside joke."

"Now you have to tell me," I insist, her easy humor causing my lips to tilt with a small smile of my own.

"We started calling him that in college. After Ted from *How I Met Your Mother*. He was always the incurable romantic, searching for the one." A soft smile plays across her face. "He called Camden and me, Lily and Marshall. Renee was our Robin. We were like a live action version of the show."

Renee was our Robin. As in Robin who ends up with Ted. Was Renee destined for Miles? He's always been adamant that there was nothing romantic between the two of them, other than that one night. Now I'm not so sure.

"So, Miles and Renee were close?" I push.

Shannon startles at my question and understanding

is written all over her face. "God, not like that," she reassures me. "Honestly, they were only ever friends. There was never even a hint of anything else." She sighs sadly. "That night was so out of character for both of them. Cam thinks it's silly, but I like to think it was the universe's way of making sure we got to keep a little piece of Renee after she was gone." She looks at me, a watery sheen to her eyes. "It probably is stupid, but it makes me feel better."

I reach across the table and grasp her hand, squeezing it gently. "I don't think it's stupid at all."

She clutches my hand gratefully. "Anyway, I think Miles felt like it was his only shot at getting his happily ever after. He was exhausted, working himself to the bone trying to balance fatherhood and work and he wasn't making good choices." She purses her lips and her eyes narrow angrily. "He didn't deserve what they did to him."

I'm about to agree with her when there's an almighty shriek from the other side of the yard and I look up to see Lulu glowering at Tyson.

"Give it back, you fuckhead!" she screams, her words loud and clear.

A shocked gasp slips past my lips. There was definitely no misunderstanding that.

Tyson's face crumbles and he starts crying just as Miles comes storming outside.

"Tallulah Renee Kent, get your butt over here, *right now*."

She spins around, turning her death glare to Miles and looking completely unmoved by his tone.

Then, as though a switch has been flicked, she begins bawling too. "He-he too-took my balloo-loon," she stutters between sobs.

"I don't care, you do not use language like that. I think it's time for you to have a nap." He begins to walk toward her, and she immediately drops to the ground, screaming and flailing her arms and legs around like crazy.

My eyes are round, and I'm pretty sure my mouth is open wide in horror.

"What's wrong with her?" I turn to Shannon who is watching everything unfold with a grin. "Is she hurt? She sounds like she's hurt."

"Nope, she's just being a normal three-year-old. I swear they demonize two-year-olds and hype up the terrible twos, but in my experience, three is so much worse."

I watch Miles bend down and scoop Lulu up, expertly avoiding her thrashing limbs. He carries her like a football, tucked under his arm, restraining her arms and angling her legs away from his body.

Her face is beet red and she continues to screech as Miles makes his way inside.

A loud laugh directed my way drags my attention from the now-closed back door to Shannon.

"Oh God, your face," she sputters.

"Does she do that a lot?" The sound of her screams still echoing in my ears.

"A normal amount."

"That's normal?" I can't hide the doubtful note in my voice.

"Yep." Shannon pops the P. "That wasn't even that bad. When Brianna was younger, she would set all the dogs off in the neighborhood with her shrieking."

My silence must speak volumes because Shannon loses it, laughing uproariously.

"What's so funny?" Camden appears and leans down to place a kiss on his wife's head.

"I think Lulu just sent Charlie running for the hills."

"That was nothing." He scoffs. "Do you remember the time Tyson lost his shit at the mall?" Camden turns to me with a smirk. "This one." He points at Shannon. "Calmly moves away from us, sidles up to the group of people who were gawking and says, 'I wonder where his mother is, she should be ashamed' and then walks away leaving me to handle both kids and the crowd."

Shannon rolls her eyes. "I stand by my actions and I'd do it all over again."

I giggle just as Miles joins us, looking completely wrung out. He flops into the chair next to me and rests his hand on my thigh, giving it a squeeze.

"I guess you finally got to meet Lulu's alter ego. We call her Annabelle."

I laugh at his comparison to the demonic doll from the horror movie.

"Tyson has crashed on the sofa," he informs Camden and Shannon. "And Bri is still on her tablet."

They nod in unison and the three of them start chatting about a local animal shelter adoption day that is coming up soon.

"I'm thinking about getting a dog. Lulu's been asking for ages and she's wearing me down."

"Don't do it," Camden argues. "It's like having another child. Ain't no one got time for that."

"You're a vet," I chastise. "Shouldn't you have a menagerie at home?"

"Don't even bother." Shannon groans. "I've been trying to talk him into a dog for years. His heart is made of stone."

"Well, I think you should get Lulu a dog. I wanted a pet so badly when I was a kid, but I was never allowed one."

Miles reaches over and kisses my shoulder, giving me an understanding look.

As though my thinking about her has conjured her up, my cell begins jumping about on the table in front of me, the screen displaying *MOM*.

Knowing she'll keep calling until I answer, I snatch the phone up, apologize and excuse myself.

"Hey, Mom." My stomach churning, I greet her once I'm inside, hidden away in the kitchen. I keep my voice low, so I don't disturb Brianna and Tyson in the playroom.

"Hi, baby." There's an awkward pause as I wait for her to continue.

When she doesn't, I clear my throat. "What's up, Mom, I'm kind of in the middle of something."

"You're working?" There's an edge to her voice that makes me uncomfortable and I wonder if she's been drinking.

"No, I'm with friends."

"Your boyfriend, you mean?" She spits the words out and I swallow hard, embarrassed by the sliver of fear that shoots through me. It's a leftover instinct from my childhood, I understand this, but it still leaves me unsettled.

"Yes."

"Speak up, baby girl, I can barely hear you," she barks snidely. "Do you have any idea how it felt to find out about this in a magazine? I bet you told your grandparents about this idiot."

I grit my teeth at her insult of Miles, wanting to defend him, but knowing it will just make this worse and draw it out.

"Well?" she prompts.

"Yes, I've told Nanna and Poppa."

She huffs out a bitter laugh. "Of course. Because they're the perfect ones and I'm the fuckup. Were they the ones putting food on the table or clothes on your back?"

I want to say yes, to challenge the childhood she's rewritten for me but there's really no point. So, instead, I give her the answer she wants.

"No," I whisper.

"No, that was *me*. The one you're so happy to toss aside and forget about. Well, now it's time to make it up to me."

Panic slices through me. "What do you mean?"

"The Inquisitor is offering us a lot of money to do an interview. It's scheduled for the fourth of next month."

"No." Surprise and contempt hardens my voice. "I'm not doing that."

"Charlotte, you *will* do this for me. The money

they're going to give m— us is too good to turn down. Surely, what's-his-name knows how the game is played and wouldn't expect you to turn it down."

Pain pierces my hand and I realize I have a death grip on my phone, so I consciously try to loosen it.

"There's no way in hell I'm doing that, Mom, and if you go ahead with it, you can forget about having any kind of relationship with me."

"Yeah, because that would be such a loss." She sneers and the familiar ache spreads through my chest. "Think about it carefully, Charlotte. I'm not turning down this opportunity and if I do it alone, they'll want something even juicier. And, I *will* give it to them."

My mind is working overtime, the repercussions of her threat filling me with dread. This will make things at work even harder. I'll most likely lose more clients which could be the final nail in my coffin at Harris & Erickson. Plus, the idea of being responsible in any way for destroying Miles' reputation further crushes me.

But betraying him would be worse than either of those things and I can't even consider it. Whatever hell my mother is about to rain down on us, we'll deal with it together.

I end the call without a word.

CHAPTER NINETEEN

MILES

iles: Meet me at the bar in The Bardot on West at 12.
Charlie: ???
Miles: Just do it, Chicago.

I glance at the clock on my phone. Twelve oh one. She never replied to my last message and I hope she turns up. After her mother's call, she was distracted all weekend, mentally preparing herself for whatever disaster is about to befall us.

When she explained the situation on Saturday, I was angry as fuck, but not for the reason she assumed. What kind of mother does this to her child? I'm only just starting to understand the extent of damage that woman did to Charlie, and I loathe her with a fierceness I have never felt before.

"What's a guy like you doing in a place like this?"

The question whispered close to my ear, startles me from my thoughts, and when I look up, she's there.

Long legs encased in sheer stockings, a tight black pencil skirt hugging her curves, and a crisp white blouse hiding her full tits. Her chocolate-colored waves have been tamed with a straightener and her pillowy lips are painted a shocking red.

She's looking perfectly well put together and I can't wait to mess her up.

A playful smile lights up her face and I nod toward the stool next to me, indicating for her to take a seat.

She crosses one leg over the other and I allow my gaze to linger for a moment.

"Lunch drinks?" My cock jerks against my pants at the sound of her husky voice.

"*A* drink." I hand her the White Russian I ordered for her. Just one, we'll both have to head back to work soon enough.

She laughs and the sound sets everything right in my world.

"What are we doing here, Miles?"

"I thought…" I trail off, shrugging. "Mondays suck and I thought we might be able to think of a way to make it not suck so much." I watch her expression closely, doing my best to gauge her response. "Maybe by doing something that involves a little sucking." I see the moment she realizes what I'm suggesting, and I can't contain my smirk.

"You want to get a room?" she asks breathily.

"Already got one. Want to join me?"

"God, yes."

From our seat in the bar, we have a clear view across the lobby to the bank of elevators. We gather our things, and as we stand, the doors to the closest one opens and we're both left shocked when Grayson and Adelaide slide into view. They look to be arguing over something, Gray playfully tugs a lock of Adelaide's blonde hair and she turns to walk out of the elevator, rolling her eyes. Before she gets too far away, Gray grabs her wrist and pulls her to him, crashing his mouth to hers.

Charlie inhales sharply beside me, her eyes wide.

"Did you know about this?" she asks. I shake my head but my exchange with Gray at family night a couple of weeks ago crosses my mind.

"I'm going to be near your work on Monday, you want to meet for lunch?"

"Oh, wait, Monday? Yeah, I can't."

I start to head in their direction, determined to get some answers but a delicate hand on my wrist stops me.

"They'll tell us when they're ready."

I know she's right but *fuck me*. My mind is blown.

So, instead we watch them walk across the lobby, side by side, their shoulders touching. But as they approach the exit, Adelaide takes his hand and looks to give it a squeeze before she drops it and takes a small step away from Gray, putting distance between them. They walk out of the hotel, and the minute their feet hit the pavement, they turn and walk in opposite directions, neither one of them glancing back.

We both stand there for a moment, shocked.

"Should we… maybe we shouldn't—"

"Oh, fuck no," I cut her off. "My kid brother is not cock-blocking me."

To prove it, I press my body against hers and take her mouth in a fierce kiss, tugging her bottom lip between my teeth, I run my tongue along it, tasting her need.

Her hands roam over my chest and she breaks the kiss breathlessly. "Let's go."

The five minutes it takes to get to the room feels like five days, and by the time I slide the keycard through its slot, I'm painfully hard.

We only take one step into the room before I have her against a wall and my mouth latched to her neck. She tastes so fucking good and I can't imagine myself ever tiring of this.

My hand slides down and the feel of her breast causes me to thrust against her, my need for release becoming urgent. She grabs me, squeezing my length and I grunt out a harsh groan against her skin.

I want to taste her pussy and then feel it grip me, pulsing around me while she comes, screaming my name.

Before I get a chance to do any of that, she slips out of my reach, falling to her knees.

She looks up at me, biting her lip almost nervously. What she sees must settle her nerves because in an instant her reticence is replaced with a look of need. Her nails are painted a pale purple and they stand out against my black pants, mesmerizing me as she urgently undoes my belt and lowers the zipper.

As much as I ache to be inside her, there is no way in hell I can stop this now. No way in hell I *want* to.

She pulls my pants and boxer briefs down in one smooth motion, and when my cock pops up, bobbing against my stomach, she licks her lips.

Licks. Her. Fucking. Lips.

She leans back on her heels, just looking at my dick like *she's* the lucky one in this situation. Not me, who's about to enjoy the fuck out of those vivid red lips wrapped around my cock, but her.

The moment comes to an end, and with slow, measured movements, she removes her blouse and then her bra, tossing them somewhere behind me. Next, she pulls her skirt up, so it's bunched around her waist, exposing her panty-less pussy to me.

Her eyes never leave my dick.

I have it in hand, jerking roughly, trying to control myself when she knocks my hand away. Her brows are furrowed as though she's annoyed not to be touching me. I take a small step forward and bring my cock to her mouth, gently running it along her lips. Her mouth opens and I press forward, giving her just the tip. She closes her lips around it and swirls her tongue over the thick head. Heat rushes up my spine and I push in deeper. Her cheeks hollow as she sucks me off, and when she grabs my ass, her nails digging in, and pulls me to the back of her throat, I lose control. I thread my hands through her hair, pulling it out of the way so I have the perfect view of me fucking her mouth. Her hands slide around my hips, and while one grips my shaft, stroking where her mouth can't reach, the other cups my balls. When she slides a finger lower, finding the spot that sends my orgasm forcefully rushing at me, I grit out a warning.

"I'm coming."

She pulls back, her mouth popping off my cock just as it starts pulsing in her hand, sending streams of my cum over her tits.

She slows her strokes and looks up at me, her lust-glazed expression apologetic.

"Sorry about that," she rasps out.

"About what?" My breathing is ragged, and I can't tear my eyes away from the mess on her chest.

"Not swallowing." She brings that lush fucking mouth of hers back to my dick and kisses the tip, smiling as it gives a small twitch of appreciation.

Dragging my gaze to meet hers, I shake my head and level her with a smirk.

"Charlie, your tits are covered in my cum. That just might be one of the best things I've ever seen in my life. Trust me, you have nothing to apologize for."

I stare down at her and the memory of the first time I saw her flashes through my mind. Buttoned up, her face lined with stress and giving off major stay-the-fuck-away vibes. I had every intention of doing just that when I heard her growl at the ice cream. It sounded like a puppy when it's attacking its favorite toy. Cute as fuck. The first time I made her smile, I felt the same intense warmth I feel now with her smiling up at me, pleased as fucking punch.

I should go and get her a washcloth. It would be the gentlemanly thing to do, after all.

Instead, I offer her my hand and drag her up to stand. Her chest is heaving and she's breathing fast, watching me intently with anticipation. I cup her cheek and she closes her eyes, leaning into my touch. I swallow hard, forcing the lump in my throat down.

I have no idea how I got so fucking lucky.

I release her cheek, letting my hand travel down the slope of her neck, the curve of her breast, the softness of her stomach, until I dip a finger into her slit, sliding it through her wetness.

A shudder rips through me and, just as she did moments ago, I fall to my knees in front of her. Lifting her leg, I wrap it over my shoulder, opening her up to me. She's beautiful. Her pussy is pink and perfect, her arousal sliding down her thigh. I flick my tongue out and lick it up, loving the way she quakes under my touch.

When she breathes out a ragged groan and her hands clutch my shoulders, I give up any pretense of taking this slow. I swipe my tongue along her and circle her clit. Nails dig into me, urging me on and, not one to disappoint, I lightly graze my teeth over the hard nub. She arches her back, pressing her pussy against my face. She's breathing harder, her unintelligible moans filling the room, and while I continue to tease her clit, sucking, biting, and flicking, I finger her entrance, pushing two fingers deep inside her, thrusting and curling them, searching for the spot that will send her over the edge.

She writhes against me and the overwhelming sensations leave me feeling almost drunk. The taste of her, the feel of her, the sounds she's making. I want to bottle it all so I can relive this moment any time I doubt the existence of perfection.

I slip my other hand around the curve of her ass and slide my finger to her puckered hole. She gasps and her hands move to my hair, pulling hard as her body contorts trying to lean into every one of my touches, but unable to.

My finger breaches that tight ring of muscle at the same moment I suck hard on her clit and my fingers curl inside her pussy. She inhales sharply, her body stiffening and then jerking as she comes hard, my name echoing through the room.

I slow my movements, lapping up her juices, and my hands grasp her hips, holding her in place when her body goes slack against the wall and her hands loosen their grip on my hair.

We stay that way for a long moment until a contented sigh escapes Charlie and I pull back, watching her. Her eyes are closed, and a satisfied smile ghosts her lips. She's exquisite.

"C'mon, let's take a shower." I slap her ass, startling her back to reality, and admire the glare she directs my way before she stalks to the bathroom, her swaying ass taunting me.

§

"I can't believe Addy didn't tell me about her and Grayson."

We're lying on the huge bed, dressed in our underwear, the afternoon sun is bathing the room in a muted glow through the sheer curtain. Charlie's fingers are running over my pecs, playing with my chest hair and I am savoring every second.

"Where did she say she was going?"

"She started taking an early lunch on Mondays a couple of months ago, she said she was treating herself to a weekly massage and that was the only time they could give her a regular appointment." Her hand stills and she raises wide eyes to me. "Do you think they've been seeing each other all this time? Is her massage with *Grayson?*"

"If you mean is Grayson giving her a happy ending, then I'd say yes." I chuckle.

She slaps me. "Why wouldn't they tell us?"

"I gave up trying to figure Gray out a long time ago." I play with a lock of her hair. "Are you going to tell Adelaide you saw her?"

"No." She pouts. "I'll get better mileage out of her guilt if I wait for her to tell me." An evil smirk plays on her lips. "What about you, are you going to confront Grayson?"

"Nah. I'll bust his balls after he comes clean. Right now, I need to keep on his good side so he'll watch Lulu for me in a couple of weeks. The animal shelter asked me to spay a litter of cats they just had handed in."

There's a pause and I glance at Charlie, wondering where her mind has gone.

"I could watch her. Or maybe I could help Grayson if you think it's too soon for me to do it by myself."

She sounds nervous, as though she's unsure how I'll react to her offer.

I lift her hand and bring it to my mouth, placing a kiss on her palm.

"You can have her for the day if you want to, I think she'd love that."

Her face relaxes and she curls into my side.

"I thought you were going to be in Boston for meetings with the pharmaceutical company that weekend?"

Her face immediately shutters. "I'm not working with them anymore."

"What happened?" I probe. She was so excited about that company. They were the first clients she had brought in to the firm and she was determined to work her ass off for them.

"It's not a big deal. They asked to have a different lawyer work with them."

I roll to my side so I'm facing her, my eyes examining her closed expression.

"Why would they do that?"

She sighs and the sound of it sends a chill through me. "They weren't happy with the publicity I've been getting."

"Because of me." My words are hard.

"Miles, please don't worry about this. I'm not." She presses a kiss to my mouth. "I have plenty of clients to keep me busy. Speaking of which, I need to get back to the office."

She hops out of the bed and begins dressing. I can't even enjoy the view because my attention is still wrapped up in her confession.

The career that she has busted her ass for, that means so much to her, is under threat. Because of me.

I watch her dress silently and let her kiss me goodbye with a promise to call tonight.

As soon as the door has shut behind her, I jump into action. I refuse to let our relationship destroy something so important to her.

Snatching up my pants off the ground, I pull out my phone and type a quick message to Harvey.

I'm in. Tell me when and where and I'll be there.

CHAPTER TWENTY

MILES

"You look like you're going to throw up."

I glance across at Aspen who is seated on a sofa opposite me.

She offers me a carefree smile. "It'll be over soon, just relax."

I let my eyes travel the length of her body, from her flawlessly made-up face to the red-soled stilettos on her feet.

"Why did you agree to do this show?" I'm suddenly desperate to know why this intelligent, beautiful woman would knowingly agree to be a part of something so tacky.

"Why did you?" she counters.

"I wanted to find a partner." It's my standard reply, but for the first time, I consider if it's the whole truth. "I felt like my life wasn't my own anymore. Maybe the show gave me a chance to run away for a while." The admission guts me, knowing I'm in this position right now because of my own cowardice.

"You're a good guy, Miles, and I am sorry for what happened. But this was a job for me." She frowns, a small crinkle appearing between her eyes. "As desperately as you needed an escape, that's how desperately I've been trying to get my break. It was never supposed to get so complicated." Her voice gently rebukes.

She's right. If I had just gone along with everyone and chosen one of the girls, none of this would have happened. It all comes back to me and my stubbornness. The entire shitshow that has been my life for the last year is entirely my own fault. All of the crap that Charlie has been dealing with, is on me.

"You okay, there?" Aspen gently prods.

"Yeah. Just ready to get this over with."

"Okay, guys." Jeremy, the host of this joke, takes a seat on an armchair between us. "The segment with all of the girls will make up the majority of the show, what we film now will be edited to fill the last twenty minutes." He looks across at me, his face deadly serious. "We'll go through the timeline from the show and, Miles, you'll explain yourself, tell us how you regret the way you handled everything, how great the show is, how wonderful Aspen is, yada yada yada." He rolls his eyes and, again, I question the morality of the people involved in this show and the disregard they show for people's lives and reputations.

My phone vibrates as someone in the studio screams, "Two minutes, people." I quickly check it, and when I see Charlie's name, I have to swallow down my guilt.

I didn't tell her I was coming here today. She thinks

I flew to Los Angeles for a conference. I hate lying to her, but I know she wouldn't approve. She'd tell me it was unnecessary and will just fan the flame when we should be leaving it to die.

But I can't let her career be a casualty of my fuckups and this is the fastest way I can put a stop to the treatment she's been receiving.

It ends today.

The heat from the studio lights has left me with a sheen of sweat and a petite makeup girl pats some powder onto my face as people rush around us, preparing to start filming. From the scowl on her face, I assume she's a friend of Sophie's.

"Right, are you two ready?" Jeremey looks between Aspen and me. "Let's make some magic."

Thirty minutes later I'm white-knuckling it. I have been bombarded with footage showing me sweet-talking a group of women, interspersed with behind-the-scenes footage of me complaining mercilessly about them to Sophie. I can't help but think that when they told me there were cameras everywhere, I never believed that there were cameras *everywhere*.

There's no point being honest. The party line is that I'm an asshole and that's what I'm here to confirm. No one is interested in knowing the truth about the show and how I was lied to.

"Jeremy, I am horrified by my behavior on the show. I have no excuse for what I did. I do want to make it clear that I never had a sexual relationship with Sophie Stevens, the makeup artist." Because I will *not* throw Sophie under the bus. "But that doesn't mean I didn't cross a line and behave inappropriately. I should have been opening up to the women who were there looking for love rather than Sophie."

I almost choke on the words, the idea that any of those women cared what I was doing is laughable.

A tearful Aspen sniffles across from me. "That means so much to me, Miles. I can't lie, I'm still devastated that you behaved the way you did, but knowing you weren't sleeping with her, and you admitting your behavior was awful, well, I feel like I can start to move on now." She gives me a watery smile.

If this woman doesn't win an Oscar at some point in the future, I'll eat my own shoe.

"Miles." Jeremy turns to me. "We all know you have a new lady love. Does this change of heart have anything to do with her?" A smarmy smile spreads across his face.

This is it. This is where I clear the air and make things right for Charlie.

"It does, Jeremy. I have been seeing a wonderful woman for a few months now, and she's helped me realize how poorly I treated everyone involved with the show. She's the one who urged me to make amends."

I almost laugh at that. Charlie would burn this studio to the ground before she would apologize to anyone involved in this mess. But when I look to my right and see Harvey standing beside the director, nodding approvingly, I know I've done the right thing.

"Well, we did try to get Charlotte to appear on the show tonight." They did? She never mentioned that.

"But it seems she is a little on the shy side." He chuckles and I force a laugh, wondering where this is headed. "Fortunately for us, her mother was more than happy to come and talk to us, so please welcome Karoline Reed."

A tall woman who looks to be in her mid-forties materializes from behind me and takes a seat next to Aspen. Jeremey greets her warmly, but I remain frozen. When I swing around to look at Harvey, his eyes glitter with malice and a smug sneer is painted across his face.

"Karoline, thank you for joining us tonight, can you explain why you wanted to be here?"

I examine her, trying to see any similarities to Charlie, but I can't. While Charlie's features are soft and effortlessly beautiful, this woman is the opposite. Heavy makeup covers her face and her hair is an unflattering peroxide color. She looks old and tired, when I know for a fact she is only in her mid-forties.

If I didn't know the harm she had inflicted on Charlie, I would pity her.

"Of course, Jeremy, thank you for the opportunity. I'm here because I'm worried about my baby girl. Charlotte is a weak girl who is easily manipulated. Knowing the type of man *he* is." She tosses a dirty look my way. "And seeing the way he has allowed her name to be dragged through the mud, I'm afraid she's going to be severely hurt—"

"Wait a minute," I interrupt. *Weak and easily manipulated.* Does she even know her daughter?

"No, you wait a minute," Karoline bites back. "I've known men like you my entire life. You're scum and you'll use my baby, take her for whatever you can get, and then disappear leaving her to pick up the pieces."

"You don't even know me."

"Of course I do. We *all* know you. You gave us a one-way ticket into your life when you put yourself on this show. Charlotte deserves better than you."

She's got me there.

Jeremy holds up his hands in an effort to diffuse the tension. "How about we ask Charlotte herself?"

My stomach drops and I glance around the studio expecting Charlie to appear. My relief at her nonappearance is short-lived, however.

"Do we have Charlotte on the line?" Jeremy directs his question to the director who gives him a nod. "Charlotte, are you there?"

"Uh, yes. Who is this?" Her voice is tight with suspicion and I think I might hurl.

"My name is Jeremy Pinoit, Charlotte. I'm here tonight with your mother and your boyfriend."

"Tonight? It's the middle of the day, what are you talking about? *Who* is this?"

I hear giggling in the background and despite the tension radiating through me, the sound of my daughter's laughter calms me a little.

"Charlotte, I'm the host of *Dating the DILF*, the show your boyfriend appeared on last year. I believe you're familiar with it."

She snorts out a laugh. "Yeah, I'm familiar with that piece of shit."

Jeremy's face drops and I have to bite back my first sincere laugh since I stepped foot in this studio.

"Uh, well, we're here filming the reunion show and we have your mother here who is expressing her concern about your relationship with Miles."

"I bet she is." She scoffs. "Miles, are you there?"

"Yeah," I force myself to answer. "I'm here, Chicago."

There's complete silence in the studio as we all listen, waiting to hear what she'll say next.

Instead, all we get is a dial tone when she ends the call.

❧

My hand stills on the doorknob and I take a deep fortifying breath before I open it. I've spent the entire trip home trying to get in touch with Charlie, but she has rejected every one of my calls. She sent me one quick message that contained two words. **Lulu's fine.**

I spent the four-hour flight home reliving the afternoon, choking on my regret and wondering when I'm going to stop making such shitty life choices.

It feels like so much longer than twelve hours since I last saw her and I need to get my hands on her more than I need my next breath.

The house is silent when I enter, and I check my watch seeing it's just after nine. After a quick sweep of the lower level, I find no one, so I make my way upstairs and head straight for Lulu's room.

The door is slightly ajar, and I peer in, seeing Lulu curled up in bed. She's fast asleep, clutching Pongo, her stuffed penguin, her gentle snores filling the room.

I push the door open farther and find Charlie asleep

on the floor, a pillow under her head and the ratty open-weaved blanket my mom crocheted for me when I was a kid, covering her.

I take a moment to enjoy the view. The connection they have developed these last few months surprised me, but I think it shocked Charlie even more. I still remember the look of horror on her face when I mentioned I had a kid. She tried to hide it, but it was painfully obvious she had one foot out the door the second it came up.

Fast-forward to this morning when the two of them practically kicked me out of the house so they could start their "girl's day." If I've messed this up, I'll never forgive myself.

Moving quietly through the room, I kneel down next to Charlie and gently shake her awake. Her eyes pop open with fright, her body taut, but she relaxes the moment she realizes it's me.

Without a word, she gets up and walks out of the room.

Sighing, I move to the bed and lean down to place a kiss on Lulu's head. She rolls over and mumbles something about fudging firecrackers and I hold my breath, praying she won't wake up.

When she burrows back into her pillow and her breathing evens out, I turn and follow Charlie downstairs.

I find her pacing between the kitchen and living room.

"How was your conference?" she snaps.

"I'm sorry." I slump against the island bench.

"You lied to me." Her chin wobbles and her eyes shine with unshed tears.

"I was trying to protect yo—"

"I don't need you to protect me, Miles. We're supposed to be a team. I'm *so* fucking mad at you right now."

"It wasn't supposed to happen like that." I hate how defensive I sound. "Harvey wasn't going to back off until I agreed to do it, so why keep fighting it?"

She stops pacing and turns to me. "And how exactly did that turn out for you?"

"I fucked up, okay?" I fold my arms across my chest. "I was trying to fix everything. I don't want to lose you because my life is a joke and that rubs off on you. How long would you stick around if being with me causes your life to come crashing down."

Her mouth drops and she's practically vibrating with rage.

"Who the hell do you think you are, Miles Kent? Do you really think I'm that shallow? Or that I'm not completely *in* this?" She storms toward me and the look on her face warns me not to interrupt her.

She stops in front of me, her hands on her hips. "I'm not looking for a fucking fairy tale, Miles, or some protector. I want a partner. What we have is real and messy, but it's incredible." Her voice breaks and I watch her swallow down a sob. "I'm prepared to risk it all for you and Lulu. Everything I want is different now, because of you two." She pauses, biting her lip. "But you need to let me fight my own battles and make my own choices. You need to settle for less than perfection, because that is bullshit and it doesn't exist. And I'm so scared that you're going to be so busy chasing something unattainable, you're going to ruin what we already have. I'm here, Miles, and I'm ready to love you through every damn storm, not just the perfect moments."

For the first time all day, I feel like I can breathe and I take a step toward her, only to be rebuffed when she steps back.

"But right now, I'm pissed, and you need to just let me be pissed." She snatches up her purse and heads toward the front door. "I'll call you when I'm ready to talk."

CHAPTER TWENTY-ONE

MILES

"What's up, Dad?" He's sitting at the dining table, sucking down a beer and watching me load the dishwasher. I can hear Lulu giggling in her playroom down the hall and I let the sound soothe me.

"Have you spoken to her yet?"

"No." It's been six days since she walked out on me and I've done my best to give her the space she needs but it's fucking hard.

I close the dishwasher and start it before grabbing a beer from the refrigerator and joining him at the table. "How did you do it, Dad?"

"Do what?"

"You and Mom. You guys had this perfect relationship, you never fought. If we're already having problems, maybe this isn't right for either of us." It kills me to even consider the idea.

"Jesus Christ, Miles, you're smarter than this." He points his beer bottle at me. "My relationship with your mother was exactly as it was supposed to be, and that's far from perfect. We fought all the time."

"No, you didn't." I scoff.

"Of course, we did. We just made a point of not doing it in front of you boys. Do you know how many times she made me sleep on the couch in the den? Why do you think I always had such a bad back?" He laughs.

"You always seemed so happy."

"We were happy. Nobody made me happier than your mom, but she had an awful temper. We both did." He shrugs as though he's not crushing every notion I ever had about relationships.

"That girl of yours is a keeper, but you fucked up, just like a million men before you. If you're lucky, she'll give you another chance. If you're not, then you'll crawl on your hands and knees and beg for forgiveness until you wear her down, because what you two have doesn't come along every day, and when it does, you fight for it."

I nod, letting his words sink in and I hope he's right. That I haven't fucked this up beyond repair.

"She's been FaceTiming with Lulu every day, did you know that?"

"She has?" I had no idea.

"Every day at lunchtime." He grins at me. "I think you're going to be fine."

"Daaaaaaaddddyyy! C'mere!" I roll my eyes and Dad chuckles at Lulu's demanding tone.

"Go check on her, I'm going to finish this and then I'll head home."

I clap him on the back, an unspoken thank you, and make my way to check on Lulu.

"What's up, kid?"

"My baby's head come off." She holds a decapitated doll up to me.

"It just popped off? All by itself?"

"Yup."

I choose to believe her because, really, who wants to believe their child is a doll decapitator?

Fifteen minutes later, I walk back into the kitchen expecting to find Dad ready to take off. Instead, I find him still seated at the table, hunched over with sweat beading his brow and his face pale and clammy.

"Dad?" I rush over to him. "Dad, are you okay?"

He's struggling to breathe and despite the panic that is setting in, I do my best to stay calm for him.

"Dad, I'm going to call an ambulance. It's going to be fine, okay? Don't worry about a thing."

He blinks once, long and slow and a feeling of dread knots my stomach.

Everything is going to be fine. It has to be.

CHAPTER TWENTY-TWO

CHARLOTTE

My eyes burn and hot tears trickle down my cheeks as I watch Chloe begging Lucifer not to leave her before they share their final kiss.

I hug the cushion closer to my chest, trying to calm myself. What the hell was I thinking watching this?

I grab the remote and search for *The Big Bang Theory*, needing something light and funny. I find the episode where it's flashing back to how Leonard and Sheldon became roommates, one of my favorites, and I settle back into the sofa. I'm craving something sweet, but I finished my last pint of ice cream earlier, and I'm down to my last pack of candy, so I'm rationing the M&M's.

I glance at my phone sitting on the coffee table, wanting to call Miles, just as I have every minute for the last six days. I had no intention of leaving it this long. I just needed a day to lick my wounds and indulge in some self-pity. But all day Sunday I kept replaying the moment I was ambushed on the phone. The sick feeling of panic and betrayal brought my childhood rushing back to me and all of my fears came roaring back to life.

How could he do something like that without talking to me? Let me be blindsided that way?

I pick the phone up and scroll to the last message from Miles, sent this morning.

Miles: Do you ever wonder if parallel universes really exist?

Miles: I hope I find you in every one of them.

I bite my lip in an effort to stop the tears, fighting every one of my instincts that are telling me to call him. My deliberation is cut short when I'm interrupted by loud banging on my door.

A sliver of fear shoots through me until I hear Addy's voice calling out, demanding I open the door.

I jump up, the urgency in her voice feeding my apprehension. When I fling the door open, she doesn't give me a chance to say a word.

"Grab your keys and purse, Robert's been taken to the hospital."

The automatic doors open, and we rush through into the emergency room waiting area. There are people everywhere and the organized chaos kicks my anxiety into overdrive.

Addy assured me that Grayson would be waiting for us and I scan the room searching him out. When I find him, my heart sinks. Gone is playful Gray with the unmistakable glint of mischief in his eyes. Instead, he's standing by the elevators, slumped against the wall with his red-rimmed eyes glued to his phone.

Addy runs straight to him and pulls him into a hug. Grayson sinks into her, wrapping his arms tight around her waist and burying his face into her neck. His shoulders shake slightly, and while there is not one part of me that doesn't want to get to Miles and Lulu as fast as possible, I turn my back and give them their moment.

"Charlie," Grayson's roughened voice calls me, and I move back toward them, grasping his hand and offering him a tight smile.

"Is he…" I struggle to finish the sentence.

"Yeah, he seems to be doing okay." His voice breaks and he scrubs his hands over his face. "They've been doing tests, but Dad's telling anyone who'll listen that he's fine, the grumpy bastard. We should be getting results soon."

Relief washes over me.

"Do you two want a minute? I can go up by myself."

Adelaide looks at me, suitably contrite. "I guess I owe you an explanation."

"Yeah, you do." I give her a kiss on the cheek. "We'll talk later. Where can I find them, Gray?"

"Sixth floor. Turn left as soon as you step out of the

elevator and then it's the fourth room on your right. You'll hear Dad bitching, trust me."

I give them both a hug and then make my way up, needing to get my hands on Miles and Lulu.

The elevator seems to be moving at the speed of a snail, hours seem to fill each second and the apprehension Grayson had managed to calm, takes flight once again.

It suddenly occurs to me that Miles never called me and nerves skitter along my spine. What if he doesn't want me here?

His earlier text flashes through my mind. *I hope I find you in every one of them.*

I don't know about any other universe, but he found me in this one and I won't let my stupid fears keep me from him a second longer.

As soon as the elevator doors open, I race out, following Grayson's directions. I spot Thomas first, he's pacing the hallway, his phone to his ear and Lulu balanced in his arms.

She has her head resting on his shoulder and is rubbing her eyes, looking tired and grumpy. She notices me before Thomas does and immediately wriggles out of his grasp, racing down the hall and throwing herself at my legs, holding on tight.

I see Thomas end his call and head in my direction, but I ignore him and lift Lulu into my arms.

"Hey, beautiful, are you doing okay?"

"Gramps is sick." She looks so despondent and her voice holds none of its usual spark. It breaks my heart.

"I know, baby, but the doctors are helping him."

"Charlotte."

I glance up to find Thomas right in front of me. I steel myself for whatever is about to come but he surprises me with a genuine smile.

"Thank you for being here, I know Miles will be relieved."

"Is he okay? Where is he?"

Lulu snuggles into me, burying her nose in the crook of my neck and I reach down and place a kiss on her head, desperate to give her some sort of comfort.

"He's in with the doctor, going through the results of Dad's tests. I just stepped out to take a call from Chrissy."

"Right," I murmur, unsure what to say next.

His eyes flit between Lulu and me, and for a brief moment, he fixates on her fingers that are playing with a lock of my hair.

"Look, I just want to apologize for what I said to you that night. I know you and Miles have been having some issues and if I've contributed to that in any way, then I'm sorry." His shoulders slump and a look of weariness engulfs him. "I just want him to be happy, Charlie, and he hasn't been in a very long time."

I don't have it in me to hold a grudge. It's obvious he cares about Miles, and even though he behaved like a jerk, I understand it came from a place of love.

For Miles, obviously. I barely have his tolerance. But this is a step in the right direction, and I won't throw it in his face.

"It didn't have anything to do with you, I promise.

He made a mistake and I punished him for it." I shrug. "A little too much, I think."

He opens his mouth to say something, but we're interrupted by the sound of the door behind Thomas opening and Robert's exasperated cry.

"For Christ's sake."

"For Christ's sake," Lulu mumbles against my neck, half asleep.

I glance up and get my first look at Miles in almost a week. His focus is on the chuckling doctor beside him and he looks exhausted.

Thomas heads in their direction and I follow, albeit at a slower pace, my nerves creeping back up.

I know the second he sees me. It's as though his entire body relaxes. I know, because mine does exactly the same thing. It's like I've been holding my breath and I had no clue until the sight of him forced me to exhale.

Thomas asks the doctor a question and I try to pay attention, but Miles hasn't taken his eyes off me.

"You came."

Did he really think I wouldn't? Does he not realize how head-over-heels, stupidly in love with him I am?

Shame washes over me when I realize that my disappearing act probably made him doubt that very thing.

"Of course. I'm—"

"Chrissy is going to come and get Lulu," Thomas interrupts, and when I look at him, I notice the doctor walking away.

"Thanks, Tom."

"I can take her home," I offer. "I'm already here, it makes sense."

"Are you sure?" Thomas asks. "It would be easier than Chrissy dragging the kids out this late."

"It's no trouble. I'll take Miles' car."

Miles doesn't seem convinced, but Thomas is already calling his wife to tell her to stay home.

It's just the three of us now and Miles takes a step closer to me. He looks like he wants to reach out, but he's holding himself back.

Without a second thought, I launch myself at him and wrap my free arm around his neck. He catches me and holds Lulu and me tight to him, breathing deeply.

We don't say anything, now is not the time. Now, he just needs to know he has me. For as long as he wants me, I'm his.

I check on Lulu who is fast asleep on the sofa in the playroom. Pongo tucked under her tiny hand, she's snoring softly, and I can't take my eyes off her. How she suckered her way into my heart so easily, I'll never know but I'll be forever grateful.

Not wanting to wake her, I walk back to the kitchen and sit at the island bench. There's a pint of ice cream before me, as well as an assortment of candy that I raided from the pantry. It's safe to say I've been eating my feelings for the last few hours.

I grab a Kit Kat from the bag and shove it in my mouth, considering how lucky Robert was tonight.

From what I gathered at my brief visit, he's going to walk away from this relatively unscathed and I'm so thankful. The fear that was etched on Miles, Grayson, and Thomas' faces will stay with me forever.

I hear the soft snick of the door opening, followed by quiet footsteps. There's a pause and I know Miles is checking in on Lulu, so I wait. Because I would wait for this man until the end of time. I just hope he was prepared to do the same.

"Hey." His whispered voice greets me, and I want to throw myself at him, just as I did at the hospital, but this time I'm the one holding myself back.

"Hi."

We stare at each other across the room, the silence heavy with everything unresolved and unsaid.

"I fucked up, Chicago."

"Yes." I nod, because what else could I say?

"Were you ever coming back to me?"

I want to say yes. After everything he's been through tonight, I want to give him that peace, but I can't. Because I'm a coward and have spent most of my life ruled by fear.

Without Robert's scare tonight, would I have found the courage to follow through and make that call?

"I don't know."

"Right." He bites his lip and nods before taking the last few steps across the room and sitting next to me. "You can't run every time I fuck up."

"How often are you planning on fucking up?" I snap back causing him to laugh and lean down to kiss my neck.

"I'm sure it'll be plenty." He grabs the bag of Swedish Fish and bites the head off one, chewing thoughtfully. "I won't let you go, I'll always come after you. But it sure would make things easier if you could just be mad at me while we're together."

He side-eyes me, challenging me to argue.

"How about you try not to fuck up and I'll try to yell and scream when you do, instead of running?"

"Deal." He puts down the candy and offers me his hand, waiting for me to shake it. It reminds me of the first time he did it at the supermarket all those months ago. Who would have ever imagined we would end up here?

I take his hand and shake, but he pulls me to him, and I fall off my seat just as his mouth lands on mine. His tongue sweeps through my mouth and I can taste his apology. His promise. His intent.

We spend necessary moments savoring each other, and when we pull apart, I'm breathless.

"I'm going to move Lulu to her bed. Will you stay tonight?"

I agree, and as we move wordlessly through the house, I watch him care for his daughter, and it strikes me how much I love his kindness. How huge his heart is and how rare his need to protect is.

I think I'll always rebel against that a little. I'm so used to being the protector myself, it's an odd feeling knowing someone will fight for me with the same intensity I would for them.

At the same time, I welcome it and I make a silent promise to myself to never get scared again.

He pulls his t-shirt off and climbs into bed beside me in his boxer briefs. I'm lying on my side and I watch him as he slides through the bed until he's beside me, mimicking my position. We're nose to nose, breathing each other's air and it hits me how much I've missed him.

A silent tear leaks down my cheek and he leans over and kisses it.

"Are we okay?"

"No," I whisper. "But I promise to be not okay by your side, instead of alone."

He considers me seriously. "I accept those terms."

"I'm so glad." I snort out a quiet laugh.

"I missed you."

I lift my hand and run my fingers along his jaw. His eyes are still tired, but they've regained a bit of their spark. "I missed you, too." I kiss his nose. "Is your dad really going to be okay?"

"Yeah." He sighs and rolls over onto his back. "It looks like it was angina, not a heart attack, so they're confident there will be no permanent damage. He'll need to go on medication and make some lifestyle changes." He turns his head and rolls his eyes. "Which he's thrilled about."

"I bet." I giggle. "Did you see Grayson and Addy at the hospital?"

"Did I see them? I can't *unsee* them." He pretends to shiver in disgust. "Once everyone was sure Dad was going to be okay, they excused themselves. When I went looking for them later, I found them practically dry humping in the stairwell."

"I wish I could say that surprises me, but Addy's a bit of an exhibitionist."

"Says the woman who let herself get fucked against a window." He scoffs.

"Hey!" I slap his chest. "That was a one-off."

"Really?" He rolls back to me and drops his arm over my waist, his hand grabbing my ass. "I bet it won't be."

"Dream on, ice cream hater." I scoot a bit closer. "Are we going to talk about last week?"

"If we have to," he grumbles.

"Lying to me doesn't protect me, we need to get that straight right now. You should have told me you were doing the show—"

"You would have tried to stop me."

"Yeah, I absolutely would have." I lift my hand to cradle his cheek. "But if you had insisted, I would have supported you. And I wouldn't have been so blind-sided. Do you have any idea how it felt to find out like that?"

He bends his head down and presses it to my shoul-der. "It wasn't how I intended it to happen, but I do accept that, even if everything had gone to plan, you still would have had every right to be pissed."

"And trust me, I would've been." I run my fingertips through his chest hair, enjoying the feel. "What happened after I hung up?"

"Uhhh…" He ducks his head and looks embarrassed. "I kind of stormed off the set, swearing at everyone."

I purse my lips and close my eyes, imagining how well that must have gone down. "So, basically you made everything a hell of a lot worse."

"Yeah, it's going to get a lot worse before it gets better." He turns serious. "I'm sorry it's affecting your job, Chicago. That's the last thing I ever wanted."

"It's fine." And it is. Somewhere along the line, my job became the least important thing in my life and I'm more than okay with that.

"What will you do if you lose your job?" He kisses along the curve of my neck.

"I'll find another one," I answer simply and then I stop the path of his lips. "You met my mom."

"Yeah, she's a…"

"Nightmare?" I supply, remembering Adelaide's words from all those months ago. "You know, I've spent so many years making excuses for her and trying to justify her behavior, but now? I've known Lulu for three months and I couldn't imagine ever treating her the way Mom did me. It would kill me to hurt her like that." I pause, trying to work up the courage for what I need to say next. "I don't think I can have her in my life anymore." I peer up at him, expecting him to be disgusted but all I see is understanding.

"I'll support whatever decision you make. If it helps, I think despite the awful example you had, you'll be an amazing mom to our kids." He slips a hand under the t-shirt I borrowed from him and smoothes it over my stomach.

"Our kids, huh?"

"Yep." He pops the P. "I figure we'll have four or five."

"Four or five?" I shriek, pushing him away.

He's about to dive back on me when we hear the door creak open and soft footfalls running across the room.

Lulu's head suddenly appears at the side of the bed, and she waves a pointed finger at us, glaring. "You two woke me up." She growls.

Laughing, I reach over and pull her into the huge bed, where she promptly snuggles between us.

Miles grins at me and I shake my head wondering how I got here, but so glad I did.

"We might have to invest in a lock on the door if you're serious about all those kids."

He leans over and brushes a kiss across my mouth. "I'll install it tomorrow."

MILES

en Years Later...

Charlie's ass pushes back against my cock meeting me thrust for thrust and the sight of her arched back, her face pressed into her pillow to smother her moans, causes me to drive myself in deeper, my harsh breathing filling the room.

Seconds later I feel her pussy pulsing around my cock, milking it, and I lose myself in her muffled sounds. Three short thrusts later, I'm coming hard, buried inside my wife and we ride our orgasms out together.

Pulling out, I fall on the bed beside her and give her an arrogant smirk.

"You're welcome."

"You're ridiculous," she counters.

"You're both disgusting!" Lulu bangs on our bedroom door making gagging noises. "Stop being gross and come and make us breakfast."

I look at Charlie and she looks back at me, amusement lighting her eyes.

"Is thirteen too young for her to make it on her own?" I question.

She throws a pillow at me. "We're not throwing our daughter out so you can get laid with no repercussions. Now go make my babies pancakes."

"Yes, ma'am." I duck down and take her nipple in my mouth sucking hard until she begins to writhe under me, then I quickly release it, grinning as she curses me out.

"Don't forget Addy, Grayson, and the boys are coming for dinner tonight and you promised to clean the grill today," Charlie shouts at my retreating back.

Half an hour later, I slide a huge plate of pancakes on the table in front of my family and take a seat beside Lulu. I tweak her nose and she groans, rolling her eyes.

"Thanks." She quickly fills her plate with pancakes before turning to Charlie. "Mom, can you take Jenna and me to the movies today?"

"Sure, what time?"

"Can I come too?" Juliette asks, walking into the kitchen and almost tripping over Mintie and our border collie Bridie, who are curled around each other, asleep, in the doorway.

Lulu looks at her sister, shaking her head. "Nope, you're too young."

Juliet scrunches her nose up and glares at her. "I'm six, that's not too young."

"J, I'll take you and Caleb to a movie while Lu goes with her friend."

My little man grins at Charlie around a mouthful of pancakes and syrup, looking at her as if she hung the moon.

I know the feeling well.

"Don't you have a meeting with the shelter supervisor today?"

Charlie has been the lawyer for a nonprofit animal shelter for the last five years. She got out of corporate law after Juliette was born, wanting something more flexible. The shelter job has been a dream come true for her.

"I can drop the girls off." I watch in disgust as Charlie and Lulu both smother their pancakes in ice cream and maple syrup. Ice cream. On *pancakes*. Sometimes they make it difficult to love them.

"No way," Lulu barks. "The last time you took us to the mall, you scared my boyfriend."

I take a gulp of orange juice and shake my head. "You don't have a boyfriend, Tallulah. You're too young."

"Daaaad." She groans before throwing Charlie a pleading look.

"Relax, Lu. I'll take you." She turns to me. "The meeting was rescheduled to Monday, so I'm all yours, all day."

"Really?" I waggle my eyebrows at her, loving her giggle.

"Stop it," Lulu demands. "There are children here," she chastises us, nodding pointedly at Juliette and Caleb.

"Huh?" Caleb looks up from his Spiderman book.

"Nothing, sweetheart." Charlie leans over and kisses his head, earning her another grin.

I sit back and observe everyone laughing and teasing around the table and it's like watching my heart beat outside of my body.

Ten years ago, my life changed irrevocably. It hasn't always been easy, but when I look at the family we've created, I know that every single moment of battle and redemption has been worth it and—

"Oh, for fuck's sake."

"Tallulah!"

I hope you enjoyed ***Dating the DILF***! Please consider taking a few minutes to leave a review.

Be sure to keep reading for an excerpt from my book ***Mistletoe Mistake***, book one in the *Greetings From Avondale* Series!

Would you like a **FREE** book?

Get your copy of **Rule Breaker**,
a steamy student/teacher rom com,
HERE!

SNEAK PEEK: Mistletoe Mistake by Amali Rose

"*How* do I look?"

I take a step back, narrow my eyes and sweep an appraising look along my friend's body. I want to say something nice, truly I do. In an effort to buy some time, I scan my office, letting my attention fall on the small bookshelf that holds my *Friends* Funko Pop! collection. I stare hard at '80s Chandler, as though he will somehow help me come up with a *nice* way to say what I'm thinking. Although on second thought, Chandler might not be the best character to find inspiration in.

I sigh and decide it's a hopeless cause, I put on my big girl panties and turn back to Troy.

"You know those scary Santa pictures from the '70s and '80s that do the rounds on Facebook every year?"

His face pinches in an entirely unflattering expression as he nods.

"You look like that."

Troy snatches the Santa hat off his head and throws it at me with all the aggression of a cuddly teddy bear. Which is to say, none.

"You're a bitch, Hols." He flops down onto the tiny sofa I have squeezed into my equally tiny office.

Stifling a laugh, I take a seat next to him and rest my head on his shoulder.

"What were you thinking when you volunteered to be Santa?"

His sigh fills the room. "I was thinking that if I didn't, there would be no Santa at Tahlia's kindergarten Christmas party."

I wrinkle my nose in distaste which draws a chuckle from Troy.

"Most normal people would see that as a bad thing."

"Christmas is overrated, I've explained this to you so many times." I give his bicep a squeeze and shift on the sofa so that I am facing him.

"Five-year-olds don't care about your childhood trauma, Holly. In fact, me volunteering to do *this*." He motions to the bright red suit he's wearing. "Is meant to stop Tahlia from experiencing her own trauma."

He shifts awkwardly, and I really do feel awful for him. Since the moment his daughter was born, she has been Troy and Matthew's entire world. Now, at the ripe old age of five, she has her dads wrapped around her little finger. As evidenced by jolly St. Nicholas in front of me.

"You're a good dad. Unfortunately, I think if you turn up looking like that you're going to have the opposite effect."

"Then help me." Troy groans and pushes himself up to stand in front of me. Hands on hips and his brow furrowed, I can practically smell the desperation on him.

"Okay, first things first. This" —I wave a finger at the Santa suit that looks like it was made in the same decade as those scary Santa pictures— "is ancient. Stop being such a cheapskate and spend the money to rent a decent suit." I take a minute to observe the way his mouth twitches and how he swallows hard at my advice.

"Fine. Anything else?" His tone is decidedly grumpier than it was a moment ago, and I bite my lip to hide a smile. Troy's infamous for his miserly ways, and I know the thought of spending money will be killing him.

"You need to get some padding." I eye his lanky frame critically. "You're way too skinny to pull Santa off without it."

"Jesus Christ," he mutters, yanking off the suit jacket.

"Yeah, also, maybe cut out the JC cursing. It's not very Christmassy." I smile sweetly at him.

"Bite m—"

"Knock knock," he's cut off by my roommate, Billie, who is standing at my office door. "Holly, I've got your —" Her eyes widen when she notices Troy standing there in Santa pants and a dress shirt, his short blond hair mussed, and she bursts out laughing.

"You both suck." He storms toward the door and

brushes past Billie, muttering about getting back to work.

"Is that my straightener?"

"Yeah." She steps into my office and hands it to me. "How long are you house-sitting for your brother? The apartment is quiet without you and Gypsy. No loud music playing and no dog howling along to your terrible singing." She smirks and follows me as I move to my desk, taking a seat opposite me. I sink down on my desk chair and feel the familiar ache in my back. I really need to check out that ergonomic desk chair my chiropractor was telling me about.

"You missing us already? We only left yesterday."

"Did I say anything about missing you? I said it was quiet. I *like* the quiet." She raises an eyebrow at me and I roll my eyes. It will be a cold day in hell before she admits to anything as sentimental as feelings.

"You're an ass. But thank you for bringing me this." I tap the tongs and then give my wavy brown locks a tug. "My hair is a nightmare without it."

"Not a problem." She shrugs. "So, how long?"

"Just a week. Brandon and Amy get back on the twenty-third." I pull a face. "They couldn't miss the Christmas party."

"Speaking of which, your dad asked me to tell you that he got your email about the party and he regrets to inform you that boycotting Christmas is not a valid reason to miss it this year." She shakes her head at me and a strand of fiery red hair escapes her low bun. "Just like it wasn't last year. Or the year before that."

I scrunch up a Post-it note and throw it at her. "I thought you were here as my roommate, not as Dad's assistant."

"I hate to break it to you, but we are one and the same. I'll let him know that you'll be there and you couldn't be more excited." She stands up and stretches before heading out.

"He'll never believe that," I call out behind her. Her only response is to flip me the bird.

I laugh lightly and turn back to my computer, trying to remember where I was with the birthday card design I was working on before Troy interrupted me.

Before I can get back to work, my phone rings. Noting it's the internal line, I answer with my attention still mostly on the design in front of me.

"Holly, sweetheart." My dad's voice booms down the line.

"What's up, Dad?"

"Your brother's trying to get in touch with you, but he said your phone keeps going to voicemail."

I groan and grab my cell phone out of the desk drawer, only to discover it's completely dead. "I forgot to charge it last night. Did he say what he wanted?"

"No, just that he wants you to call him."

"Okay, was that all?"

"Your email was very entertaining," he replies dryly, and a small grin plays on my lips.

"Why thank you, I try my best." I giggle.

"You know, you'll have to get over this Christmas hatred thing eventually."

"That's not going to happen. Christmas sealed its fate on my tenth birthday when no one turned up to my party because they were suffering from post-Christmas exhaustion. I was ten, Dad. Ten! Then there was the yea—"

"I remember it all, sweetie," he cuts me off mid-rant. "But Christmas is such a wonderful time of the year. It's about love and family and everything that's important." His voice softens, gaining the sentimental tone he gets when discussing any holiday.

My father is unapologetically emotional about special occasions. It's one of the things that led him to opening a greeting card company with my mother so many years ago and, while I would never say this to his face, his sentimentality has only gotten worse with age.

"I know, I know," I sigh, tiredly. We have this same argument year after year. But seriously, if your birthday was December twenty-fifth, you would resent sharing your special day too.

"I have to go, Dad, I'm in the middle of a project, but I'll talk to you later, okay?"

He relents and we say our goodbyes.

It's moments like this that I don't entirely love working at *Greetings from Avondale*. Originally a small boutique greeting card company, my parents started the business before my brother was born. It has grown and expanded over the years and is now one of the most successful greeting card companies in the US.

I always loved coming here as a child. It felt like a second home to me and when I graduated with a degree in graphic design three years ago, it was only natural I start working for the company that was such an intrinsic part of my family.

Plus, despite how I feel about Christmas, I did inherit my father's love of holidays and special occasions, and there is something almost magical about creating a keepsake for people to celebrate the most important moments in their lives.

I may hate Christmas, but I love my job.

"C'mon." I jiggle the key in the lock and mentally cross my fingers that it will work this time. Brandon warned me that this lock was sticking. He promised he would fix it before they left, but I guess he didn't get around to it. Ugh, which reminds me, I never called my brother to see what he wanted. I sigh, hating how the day got away from me. I can hear Gypsy on the other side of the door, sniffing around and scratching at the door to get to me. Finally, with one last jiggle and a silent prayer, the key turns and the door swings open. I trek through the mudroom, into the kitchen and dump my things on the island counter, before crouching down and greeting my fur baby with ear scratches and a tummy rub. When she's suitably loved up, she gives me a final lick and races off to her toys where she busies herself with a tennis ball.

Groaning, I roll my shoulders and slump onto the counter, considering what to do for dinner. Deciding that a grilled cheese will have to do, I'm halfway to the refrigerator when I remember the spa bath Brandon and Amy had installed in their bathroom earlier this year and suddenly my plans for the night change. I grab a glass and a bottle of wine—*Moscato, my favorite, thank you Amy*—from the refrigerator and I head toward the stairs, already fantasizing about sinking into a tub full of bubbles.

I've barely made it three steps when my newly charged phone starts buzzing in my purse. I groan and try to decide whether or not to ignore it. Guilt stops me, knowing Brandon will most likely be annoyed he's been chasing me all day, so I turn back to the counter and search through my bag until I find it. Unexpectedly seeing my friend Tessa's name on the screen, I answer the call and greet her warmly. After a few minutes of small talk, I grab the wine with my spare hand, and pivot back in the direction of the stairs, figuring I'll switch to speaker and finish the conversation while I get my bath ready.

"Anyway, I'm calling about book club." Tessa's usually melodic voice sounds worried.

"What's up?" I take the stairs two at a time, eager to reach paradise. I can already feel the tension start to leave my body, imagining my body sinking into the hot water.

"I know we were supposed to have our next meeting at my apartment, but I've had a business trip sprung on me, so I'm going to be out of state until the twenty-third."

My feet hit the landing and I turn toward the bathroom.

"Oh, that's no problem, Tess. Billie and I can host it this time and you can FaceTime us."

"You're sure?"

"Of course." I reach for the bathroom door and open it, already planning the night in my head. "Our place is p—p—penis!"

NICK

I should probably cover my dick.

She hasn't taken her bright blue eyes off it since she flung open the bathroom door, and that was at least thirty seconds ago.

Thirty long, *silent* seconds ago.

The little fucker seems to be getting off on her attention though, because it twitches, and her round eyes get even wider.

Yeah, I really should cover my dick.

"Hey, Holly." I continue to scrub the towel over my hair.

My voice seems to startle her, and I wish I could adequately describe the sound she makes. Imagine a strangled screech, some garbled words and a deep exhalation of breath. Now imagine all three mixed together, and you might come close to the sound I just experienced.

I'm not going to lie, my cock has never gotten a reaction like that before and I'm not mad about it.

Taking pity on her, I lazily wrap the towel around my waist and turn to face her, scratching my pec as I do. A sparking sensation under my skin follows the path of her eyes and I realize I might be in trouble.

"Sorry, I should have locked the door. I was filthy and in a rush to clean up. I wasn't thinking." My apology is half-assed because I can't count the number of times I've imagined her eyes on me like this.

A small squeak escapes her full, pink mouth, reminding me of a cartoon character, and she abruptly turns, making her escape back the way she came.

Well, that could have gone better.

Ten minutes later I walk into the kitchen to find Holly pacing back and forth, her arms wrapped firmly around her waist and her bottom lip clamped between her teeth.

I would also like to point out that I am now fully dressed. Winning at life, right here.

"You okay?"

She startles at the sound of my voice before turning to face me. The scorching sensation under my skin fires back to life.

This is definitely going to be a problem.

"Yeah." She smiles ruefully. "Sorry about that, I didn't realize you were here."

"I guess Brandon didn't tell you he said I could stay for a few days?" I make a mental note to kick my best friend's ass.

Something akin to understanding lights up her eyes. "He was trying to call me today, but we didn't connect." She shakes her head and mutters something under her breath that I don't quite catch.

"Ah, well, there's some plumbing problems at my apartment and I needed a place to stay for a couple of days. Brandon said it would be okay for me to crash here." I grimace before continuing. "I hope that's okay? I can always find a hotel…"

"Of course it's fine! Um, I guess we don't both need to be here though." Her brows pull together and a cute little line appears. "I can go back to my apartment until you're gone." She gives her head a little nod, as if it's decided.

Fuck no.

"Don't do that." Shit, that might have come out slightly more aggressive than I meant it to, because her head instantly pops up, looking at me with surprise written all over her face. "I just mean, I'm only going to be here a couple of days. You'll only just finish unpacking and it'll be time for you to come back. You might as well stay."

"I guess that's true." She nibbles her lip. "All right, I guess being roomies for a couple of days won't kill me." Moving toward the island, she takes a seat on one of the uncomfortable-looking stools. "Have you eaten? I'm starving."

A bark sounds from the mudroom and her little dog comes rushing out and drops a ball at my feet.

"I can always eat." I bend down and scoop up the furball who starts wriggling in my arms and trying to lick my face. "She's not much of a guard dog, you know." I sit on the stool next to her—FYI, they're just as uncomfortable as they look—still trying to wrangle the brown and white dog. "When I got here, all she did was sniff me and claw my legs until I picked her up."

Her face softens as she watches Gypsy, who has turned her attention to Holly and is trying to jump from my arms to hers.

"Yeah, the only way she'll ever stop an intruder is by licking them to death." She wraps her arms around the fluffball, places a kiss on the top of her head, and then leans down to place her on the ground. Picking up the ball Gypsy dropped, she throws it back toward the mudroom and we both watch her race after it, her claws clattering on the hardwood floor.

"Is pizza still your favorite? The local place is pretty fast, we can probably be eating in under an hour."

My ego gives a fist bump, realizing she remembers my favorite food. Which is ridiculous. I practically lived here growing up. Just because she remembers I love pizza doesn't mean anything.

"Yeah, pizza's great."

I watch her tap away on her phone, placing the order. Her other hand plays with a strand of her long hair and her normally wide eyes are narrowed as she stares at the screen. Her creamy skin has a perpetual rosiness along her cheekbones and she still has a smattering of freckles across her nose, just like she did when she was a kid.

I think back to the last time I saw her. It was her twenty-first birthday and I remember the exact moment I spotted her. She was moving through the room confidently, her face lit up with a huge smile, and it was like a punch to the face. The fresh-faced kid I remembered from five years earlier was gone and had been replaced by a woman I wanted in my bed.

Or in my car. Really, wherever she would have me.

Her small nose scrunches up. "Pineapple on pizza is so gross, Nick."

Well, would you look at that. She even remembers my exact order.

"Pineapple and sausage pizza is a gift from the gods. You should try it."

She presses a final button and drops her phone onto the counter. "I will *never* eat pineapple on pizza and, honestly, I don't entirely trust anyone who does."

I clutch my chest, wounded. "That hurts, Holly, that really hurts." Standing up, I stretch my arms above my head, my shoulders feeling tight from a long day at work.

A small sigh catches my attention and I look down to see Holly staring at my sweatpants. She runs her tongue lightly along her bottom lip and I feel my cock twitch in appreciation.

I clear my throat and try to hide a smirk. Everything in me wants to make a smart-ass comment. Flirt with her a little. But Brandon's warning from three years ago rings loudly in my head, *"keep your fucking hands off my sister, asshole. You're not even worthy of looking at her right now."*

I'm not going to lie, the chemistry between us is unexpected. I'm well aware of the attraction I felt to her, all those years ago, but I never expected to see the same interest reflected back at me. My gut clenches and I force myself to remember how Brandon stood by me when so many others disappeared. Starting something with his sister would be a dick move.

Instead, I ignore the heated moment and move to the refrigerator to grab a bottle of water.

Her stool screeches across the floor as she stands and I watch her from the corner of my eye awkwardly rub her chest.

"I'm going to go have a shower. Can you give me a shout when the pizza arrives?"

Without waiting for my answer, she turns and hotfoots it out of the room, leaving me with only an image of her naked and sudsy, and a bad feeling about how the next few days might play out.

§

I am halfway through my second slice when Holly bounds down the stairs in a pair of ass-hugging yoga pants and a sloppy orange sweater that's falling off one of her shoulders. The scent of peppermint infuses the air around her. I shift in my seat, putting my foot on the coffee table so my leg is slightly raised and hiding my semi.

Her hand runs along the tinsel tied to the banister as she skips down and I notice her roll her eyes.

"What was that?"

"What was what?" She heads straight for the pizza

boxes beside my foot and makes a gagging noise when the first box she opens has my pizza in it.

"You rolled your eyes at the tinsel. I'm not sure what an inanimate object could have done to deserve that kind of treatment."

"It's a Christmas decoration. It deserves that treatment just for existing." She takes a seat on the other end of the couch, and sits cross-legged, balancing a paper plate with two of her own slices on her lap.

Her comment rattles a memory loose and I suddenly have an image of fourteen-year-old Holly casually strolling into her family Christmas party wearing a *Santa is Satan* T-shirt. Her horrified grandparents promptly ushered her out of the party, much to her delight.

"Oh god, Santa is Satan." I almost choke on a laugh. "I had forgotten all about that."

A small smile plays on her lips, but she folds them between her teeth in an effort to hide it. "That was one of my better efforts. Nana and Papa were horrified." She gives up on hiding her smile and giggles. "But Mom and Dad respected my dedication and let me spend the rest of the night in my room." She grimaces at me. "The grandparents were *not* impressed with that."

We both go back to our food and, maybe it's just me, but there's an awkwardness between us that I hate.

It's funny, Holly and I have known each other most of our lives, but I can't remember a single time we have spent time alone like this.

Brandon and I became inseparable the day the

Curtises moved in next door to my family when we were eight. Since my parents worked so much we spent most of our time at his house. His mom was like a second mother to me, and even though his dad worked a lot, he was still around more than mine.

My memories of Holly aren't so clear though. I remember being curious about her when they first moved in. Being an only child, I wasn't sure how to behave around a little sister, which is how I assumed I should treat her. I always followed Brandon's lead, teasing her and playing jokes. But the older she got, the less she was around. In fact, the last few years before I left for college, it felt like she was leaving every room I entered.

I remember the dread I felt at the time, worried I had upset her. Selfishly concerned that it would mean my presence in their home would become unwelcome, and I'd have to go back to spending my nights in my own house. Where the laughter and warmth of the Curtises' would be replaced with silence and emptiness.

Brandon waved off my concerns and assured me it was nothing I had done. I had no reason not to trust him, so I did.

Her awkwardness now though, has all those doubts resurfacing, although this time for very different reasons.

I snag another couple of pieces of pizza and swing my legs up onto the sofa, nudging Holly's knee with my toes.

"What's the deal with hating Christmas? I feel like I

need to bah humbug you and pelt you with candy canes."

She immediately perks up. "Do you have any candy canes?"

"No." I laugh.

Her blue eyes narrow with a glare. "You really shouldn't get people's hopes up like that, you know."

"So, you're not against all Christmas traditions then? Good to know." I take a bite of pizza and watch her try to stutter a reply before taking pity on her. "I get it, if my birthday was Christmas Day, I'd hate it too."

She chews slowly and eyes me suspiciously. Whatever she sees on my face must soothe her, because she shrugs and looks away.

"It's childish and petty, I'm fully aware of that."

"Nah, everyone wants to feel special on their birthday." Honestly? I have no idea if that is true. I couldn't give a fuck about my birthday, but I'm not liking the look of unease on her face and I'll say anything to get rid of it.

"It's just" —she tosses her empty paper plate on the coffee table and turns to face me fully— "your birthday and Christmas are supposed to be the most magical days of the year when you're a kid." She pauses, chewing on her lip and staring off, just above my head. "But when your birthday is *on* Christmas, you kind of lose the magic of both days. Your birthday isn't special because everyone is too wrapped up in the holidays to really care about it, and then your resentment of Christmas steals the joy of *that* day. It's like you lose the magic of your childhood way too soon and it's just sad."

She exhales out a deep breath and groans. "God, that sounds so dramatic, ignore me." Shaking her head, she swipes the television remote off the table and turns the TV on.

I sit, staring at her, completely enthralled and a little heartbroken for Holly, the little girl who never experienced the same joy I did in my childhood.

My parents worked their asses off to give me the life they felt I deserved, so they were gone a lot. Too much, and I spent a lot of years angry at them for that. But my birthday and Christmas were the two days a year I could always count on them being there, from sunup to sundown. They were my favorite days of the year, and I hate that she never experienced the pure happiness those days are supposed to give children.

Holly leans forward, her eyes glued to the TV as she flicks through the channels, completely oblivious to the plan that is currently forming in my mind.

A plan that does not bode well for my promise to stay away from my best friend's sister.

"Holly," I start, grabbing her attention. "I have a proposal for you."

Mistletoe Mistake is AVAILABLE NOW!

Stay Connected

Private Facebook Group: https://www.facebook.com/
groups/amalisrisqueromantics
Instagram: https://www.
instagram.com/authoramalirose
BookBub: https://www.bookbub.com/
authors/amali-rose
Amazon: https://www.amazon.com/author/amalirose
Facebook: https://www.
facebook.com/authoramalirose
Goodreads: https://www.goodreads.com/author/
show/17064277.Amali_Rose

My newsletter is the best way to stay in contact with
me! You'll get first look at titles, covers and release
dates, plus exclusive sneak peeks!
Sign up here: https://tinyurl.com/y6h3hw9s

More by Amali Rose

Finding Forever Series
(Standalone series)

Under the Cherry Blossoms >> Fling to Forever Romance
Dandelion Dreams >> Enemies to Lovers/Office Romance
Amongst the Wildflowers >> Friends to Lovers Romance
Breathing Wisteria >> Second Chance Romance
Finding Forever >> The Complete Series

Greetings From Avondale Series (Standalone Series)

Mistletoe Mistake >> Brother's Best Friend/Holiday Romance
Miss Independent >> Billionaire Romance

Standalones:

Dating the DILF >> Single Dad Romantic Comedy

ACKNOWLEDGMENTS

As always, to every blogger who has ever read, reviewed, shared or supported me in any way, you have my complete gratitude and I will never take it for granted. *Thank you, thank you, thank you!!!*

To the person reading this… thank you for taking a chance on my words. I put my heart into every story I write and putting them out there into the world is just as terrifying today as it was with book one! I hope this didn't disappoint.

Kim, your friendship, support and honesty makes all of this a little bit easier. Thank you!

Antonette and Rachel, thank you for always having my back. I'm lucky to have you both in my life.

To every one of my friends, family and loved ones, who support me and cheer me on, you make me brave and I adore you all for it.

Writing a book can be a very solitary experience, but *publishing* a book takes a whole team. If you're lucky, you find a group of people who care about your story as much as you do. *I have been so. Incredibly. Lucky.*

My alpha/betas: Kim, Rachel, Tamara & Tre, thank you for putting up with my always-behind-schedule-but-even-more-behind-than-normal ass. Your input and honesty helps make me better, and I'm so incredibly thankful to all of you.

Ellie McLove (My Brother's Editor), thank you for putting up with my inability to meet a deadline or learn where to put a damn comma. Please don't ever leave me!

Judy Zweifel (Judy's Proofreading), there is no one I would rather give my manuscript it's final polish. Thank you for always explaining your changes so I can learn and being prepared to google the Aussie slang that sometimes slips through!

Stacey Blake (Champagne Book Design), thank you for taking my manuscripts and turning them into a real-life book of beauty! I'm so grateful to you.

Ben Ellis (Tall Story Designs), working with you is a joy! Thank you for putting up with my ramblings and somehow turning them into a work of art. My books are made better by your remarkable covers.

Kylie McDermott and Jo Webb (Give Me Books), you are the most amazing PR team! Your kindness is equal only to your professionalism and I hope we work together on many, *many* future projects!

Last, but certainly not least, my street team, *Amali's Sinful Sweethearts*! Antonette Santillo, Cassy Kubehl, Devon Farrow, Heather Poll, Katrina Haynes, Kristi Smith, Lauren Harwood, Rachel McLean, Tamara

Harrington & Tre Talbot. What would I do without you?! Thank you for your constant hard work, support and encouragement. I'm keeping you all forever!!!

Huge love & hugs!
Amali xox

ABOUT THE AUTHOR

USA Today Bestselling author Amali Rose is a former blogger from Australia, who released her debut novella in 2017.

A self confessed bookworm, her love affair with the written word began as a child, with *The Magic Faraway Tree*. Her tastes have grown and evolved over the years and, after stumbling into the indie community a few years ago, she discovered her passion for romance with a side of smut.

When not reading or writing, Amali enjoys cheesy pop music, netflix marathons, and she believes strongly that pink, puppies and chocolate make the world a better place!